banway 3/11/94

"Oh, how am I going to make you pay attention?"

Kerry inhaled deeply on the cigarillo. "I assure you, chérie, you have my complete and total attention."

He exhaled a perfect ring. Lucinda's scowl turned into a smile as she waved her arm through the smoke without disturbing the circle. Kerry blinked. "Excellent, ma'am, although I did have more in mind than parlor tricks."

"I know, touch me."

"At last."

Now a gentleman would have reached out in a gentle caress along her cheek, or a soft stroke on her bare upper arm. Stanford was well past the stage for gallantry. He _____ ____ wrap his hand around those _____ ____ globes that u_____ _____ bodice of her _____ _____. His fingers ti___ _____ g in them. Nothing.

AN ANGEL
FOR THE EARL

Barbara Metzger

FAWCETT CREST • NEW YORK

Sale of this book without a front cover may be unauthorized. If this book is coverless, it may have been reported to the publisher as "unsold or destroyed" and neither the author nor the publisher may have received payment for it.

A Fawcett Crest Book
Published by Ballantine Books
Copyright © 1994 by Barbara Metzger

All rights reserved under International and Pan-American Copyright Conventions. Published in the United States of America by Ballantine Books, a division of Random House, Inc., New York, and simultaneously in Canada by Random House of Canada Limited, Toronto.

Library of Congress Catalog Card Number: 93-90720

ISBN 0-449-22215-2

Manufactured in the United States of America

First Edition: March 1994

To Ruth Cavin, Harvey Klinger,
Barbara Dicks, and Melinda Helfer.
Thank you.

Chapter One

Miss Lucinda Faire was eloping with the man
of her dreams. Captain Leon Anders was abducting
one of Derby's leading heiresses. Obviously, this
was not a marriage of true minds.

Lucinda's first inkling that her dreams were
about to be shattered came when the handsome
officer ignored her company in the hired coach in
favor of the silver flask he pulled from his scarlet
coat. Not only was Leon drinking in front of a
lady, but he had not thought to provide his beloved with anything to ward off the morning chill
in the damp, drafty carriage. Having crept from
her house before first light, Lucinda naturally
hadn't broken her fast. She would not complain,
though, lest dear Leon think her the peagoose she
undoubtedly was for not even saving a roll from
her dinner to carry along the way. Of course a
kind word from dear Leon would have warmed
her to the core, the way his sweet whispers always did in their stolen moments together. He
must be too concerned with their flight to Gretna,
she excused him, or perhaps all gentlemen were

that cranky in the morning. Heaven knew her father was.

Lucinda settled back in her corner of the coach, a smile on her lips, prepared to enjoy every moment of the grandest adventure of her seventeen years. No, she amended, this was the *only* adventure in her seventeen constricted, confined, and uncompromisingly correct years. Her parents had seen to that, the same way they were seeing to her marriage to Lord Halbersham, an ancient, curmudgeonly neighbor who spouted piety while his servants went cold and hungry.

Which reminded Lucinda of her present discomfort. "Leon, do you think we might stop soon to refresh ourselves? Perhaps at the next change?"

"What, are your attics to let?" her beloved growled. "Do you want your father to find us before nightfall?"

Well, no, but she couldn't help thinking that ten minutes spent sipping a cup of hot tea and ordering warm bricks for their feet would not make that much difference. Her father wouldn't even think to look for Lucinda until she did not arrive promptly for the noon meal, so sure was he that she'd be at her chores or practicing the harp. She drew her serviceable gray wool cloak more snugly about herself and studied her adored Captain Anders.

For once the sight of her soon-to-be-spouse did not send chills down Lucinda's spine. Perhaps that was because there were already so many chills down her spine and elsewhere, one more couldn't be noticed. Or perhaps the dark stubble on his jaw and the bloodshot cast to his eyes lent him an unfamiliar, harsh look. Lucinda was only used to the fair-haired, blue-eyed Adonis who had stolen her heart that day at the haberdasher's when he smiled just for her, plain little Lucinda Faire.

Leon was not smiling now, nor when they finally stopped to change the horses close to midday, and

Lucinda made to follow him from the coach into the posting house.

"Get back in there, you nodcock," he snapped, looking over his shoulder at the busy inn yard. "Do you want to chance being recognized this close to your home? One more red-coated soldier won't draw anyone's attention, but think of your father coming to ask after a blondish chit in a gray cloak, for pity's sake." Lucinda's hazel eyes had grown wide in her face at his abrupt speech, so Captain Anders drew his gloved hand down the side of her cheek. "Hush now, sweetings. I'll bring back a nuncheon fit for a princess. My own princess." That won him back a weak smile, so he shut the door behind him, adding, "I am only thinking of your reputation."

Then why hadn't he pulled the window shades? Lucinda could not help wondering. And worrying about her reputation in the middle of a scandalous elopement seemed just a tad hypocritical. She tried her best to bury such disloyal thoughts. Dear Leon was simply as nervous and anxious as she was. This eloping business was not nearly as romantical as she'd imagined.

Captain Anders must have refilled his flask at the inn, for he kept sipping at it during the long afternoon, slouched in his corner across from her. As the bricks at her feet cooled off, Lucinda stared at the bleak, wintry countryside rather than at the reddening, scowling face of her beloved. Finally she fell asleep, huddled in her cape.

"Wake up, Lucinda." Leon was shaking her shoulder none too gently. "We're at the inn where we'll spend the night."

Lucinda shook her head to clear her mind, dislodging a pale curl or two. "But ... but it's still light out. We can travel for another hour at least and gain that many miles on my father's pursuit."

"These horses are tired and the driver says there is not another suitable inn for hours more. We'd be

3

forced to put up at a hedgerow tavern or some such."

"But that means we'll be two nights on the road, not one, without even a maid to chaperone. You were so concerned about my reputation at luncheon, what—"

"I said this is where we'll stay, dash it. Don't argue, you plaguey chit. Now, get down, and fix your hair. You look like a schoolgirl."

Stunned and still sleep-fuddled, Lucinda could only stumble after him. He took her arm as they passed the innkeeper, smiled as the man bowed, and hustled her up the stairs.

"There was only the one room, so I said we were man and wife. Less explaining that way, anywise."

"But I cannot share the room with you!"

He ignored her squawked protest. "Less expense, too. I ain't made of brass, you know. How much blunt did you bring along anyway?"

Lucinda reached into her reticule. "Just what's left from my pocket money. You know Father does not give me an allowance or anything." She held out a handful of coins. "Will it be enough for another room?"

He took the coins. "We're on our way to Gretna, blast it, so stop being so deuced missish. I can't abide a prosy female."

"Leon, I . . . I think you may have had too much to drink."

"And what would you know about it, Miss Prunes-and-Prisms? Oh, go take your cloak off and sit down. The innkeep promised dinner soon. Try to act like a starry-eyed bride and not some frightened fawn, or he'll throw us out." The captain shrugged out of his uniform coat without a by-your-leave and tossed it onto the bed before sprawling into the room's only comfortable-looking chair.

Lucinda picked up the scarlet jacket and hung it in the clothespress with her cloak. At least the room appeared clean, boasting a linen-laid table, and chairs, and even a vase of flowers on the stone mantelpiece. Best of all, there was a sofa near the fireplace. A sofa that looked too short for Leon's tall frame, she noted with a twinge of satisfaction, thinking of the uncomfortable night he'd have in store.

Once again Lucinda's and the captain's thoughts were not marching in step.

"You're going to sleep where?" she gasped after dinner when he'd made his plans evident. "Not on your life!"

"Come on now, sweetings. What can a night or two matter?" He was holding her in his arms, stroking her back, whispering in her ear.

Perhaps a night or two in anticipation of their vows was not such a big thing after all, Lucinda was starting to think, when the captain kissed her. His mouth was wet and cold, and smelled of wine and brandy. It mattered. A lot. He was holding her so tightly she felt suffocated. She pushed him away. "No," she declared, shoving him away again when he dragged her back into his embrace and started drooling wet kisses on her neck. For a girl's first experience at lovemaking, this left something to be desired. Not only did her hero seem to have feet of clay, but those feet were set in quicksand.

"Come on, sweetings." Leon was panting. "We have to make sure you're well and truly compromised before your father finds us, else he's liable to drag you back home and hope to scotch any rumors."

"Stop that, Captain!" Lucinda slapped away a hand that was straying where no man's hand had ever strayed. "And I do not wish to be compromised. In fact, I am thinking that perhaps we were too hasty about this elopement after all. We should have gone to my father, explained your prospects—"

"What prospects were those, sweetings?" he asked with a sneer. "Everyone knows the only

5

prospects I have are hopes of getting your skint of a father to part with some of his blunt."

The sinking feeling in Lucinda's stomach had nothing to do with the inferior dinner she'd just eaten. "My father's money? You . . . you don't love me at all, do you?"

"Don't come the innocent with me, girl. You would have come away with anyone who saved you from old Halbersham."

"No, I lo—" Miss Faire's pride kept her from uttering the fatal words. She raised her chin. "I have reconsidered. I no longer wish to marry you, compromised or not."

He laughed. "Who's talking of marriage? You think I intend to marry a drab little dumpling of a chit like you? You're even greener than I thought."

Lucinda still hadn't grasped the depths of his infamy. "You planned this whole fake elopement just to ruin me?"

"That's only incidental, and no great treat either, I can tell you," he said, adding insult to injury, waving his hand vaguely at her limp blond hair, the plain gray traveling dress that did nothing to improve a short, squat figure. The captain's lip curled in derision. "And they say there's no such thing as a homely heiress."

She slapped him. "You, sirrah, are no gentleman. I am going home."

Rubbing his cheek with one hand, the captain shoved her into a chair with the other. "You're not going anywhere until your father gets here with my blunt. That's right, I left him a note explaining right where you'll be and how much he'll have to pay to get you back, and to keep my lips sealed."

"My father will make you marry me," Lucinda cried, horrified at his admission, dismayed at the thought of spending the rest of her life with such a villain.

"Not when I show him my marriage lines. My Fiona's waiting for me in Liverpool."

"Then he'll kill you."

"That old man? He can challenge, but I'm a crack shot."

If she had a pistol, Lucinda thought she might use it herself. "He'll have you arrested for abducting a minor. He'll . . . he'll ruin your career." Lucinda was running out of dire threats.

Anders just snickered and raised a bottle to his lips. Some of the wine dribbled out the side of his mouth. "Think again, little dab, he'll never make more of a scandalbroth by calling for the constables. And my army career has been over for years. The uniform just made my new, ah, profession more successful."

Cardsharping, usury, highway robbery? Lucinda didn't even ask. "My father will see that you never get away with this. And you won't get a farthing out of him."

"Oh, he'll pay. They all do."

All? Lucinda choked back tears of rage and heartbreak. She'd been seven kinds of fool, but she wasn't going to make it eight by staying here one second longer.

Once more Miss Faire and her erstwhile fiancé had a major difference of opinion. As usual, the opinion of the stronger personality, or the stronger person, held sway. Anders dragged Lucinda back from the door by a fistful of the unfashionable gray gown, which ripped down the front as she wrenched out of his clasp. She was crying in earnest now, fear suddenly mingling with the welter of emotions. "Let me go!" she screamed when he grabbed for her again, trying to hit him, claw him, kick him, bite him, anything to get away.

"Shut up, bitch." He slapped her, jerking her head back. Lucinda screamed, and thought she heard hollers in the hallway so she screamed again. Leon shook her, hard, then pressed his slimy lips to hers.

Lucinda pushed him away with all her strength,

7

which was nothing compared to the captain's, except that he was the worse for drink and unsteady on his feet. He staggered back, cursing loudly. Then his foot struck the bottle he'd dropped. He toppled backward with a yell that was abruptly replaced by a sickening thud as his head hit the corner of the stone mantelpiece. Captain Anders collapsed the rest of the way to the floor while Lucinda shouted his name.

"Leon? Captain? My God, Leon, you can't be dead!"

The dirty dish won that argument, too.

The room was filled with people almost before Captain Anders hit the floor. The innkeeper was shouting for boys to ride to the doctor, the magistrate, the undertaker. His wife was squealing about never having such goings-on under her roof, and death being bad for business, and she should have known such a handsome rogue had no decent business with any milk-and-water miss. One of the maids fainted, two of the lady guests called for their carriages and reckonings, and a young buck who'd been in the taproom swore he'd heard the whole thing and was just about to rescue the young lady. The merchant in the room next door concurred the dastard had got what he deserved, but never mentioned a thought about coming to the damsel's aid.

And there was blood everywhere. On the floor, on the hearth, on Lucinda's hands, on her gown, on her mouth where he'd struck her. And mostly there was blood spattered all over Leon, so someone covered him up with a blanket from the bed. No matter; Lucinda still saw him. Someone put another blanket around her shoulders to cover up her torn dress. Someone else, one of the messengers, she thought, or perhaps the doctor, put a glass into her hand. She drank.

Then the magistrate came and asked a great

many questions, which everyone else seemed to want to answer.

"I killed him," she interrupted in a voice as dead as the captain. "My name is Lucinda Faire, of Fairview Manor, Derby. I did not mean to, but I killed him."

"No, you didn't, my dear," the magistrate replied. "The fireplace killed him. You were only trying to get away, self-defense and all that." The magistrate was only a local squire. He was not about to set himself up against Sir Malcolm Faire, the richest man in Derby, not over some loose screw who should have hung for his crimes. After all, the magistrate had daughters of his own. "Death by misadventure, we'll call it. There'll have to be an inquest, but don't worry, your papa will come and handle all the details. I already sent for him. Why don't you wait downstairs in the private parlor? You'll be more comfortable there than up here with the, uh, mess."

Her father was coming. The magistrate had sent for him; Leon had sent for him. Leon did not love her; her father did not love her either, but he was her father. He'd take her home, where she could burn this gown and have a bath to rid herself of the stench of Leon and this place and the blood. Nanny would put something on her cut lip. But there was no reason for Sir Malcolm to see Leon or this second-rate inn or the blood. Sir Malcolm hated anything tawdry or unkempt, anything that did not fit into his orderly universe.

So Lucinda decided to go home. She was bound to meet up with her father on the road, and anything was better than staying here, with Leon upstairs. The blanket still around her shoulders in lieu of her cape, Miss Lucinda Faire walked out the unattended front door of the inn, gathered the reins of a horse left tied there in the excitement, mounted with the aid of a handy barrel, and rode into the pitch-black night.

The doctor was not hopeful. "She is badly concussed from the blow to her head when she fell off the horse, and then there is the congestion of her lungs from lying out in the cold all night and half the day. The most worrisome, however, is that your daughter has not regained consciousness for two days. I fear that the shock from the other, ah, unfortunate events have sapped her will to live. Coupled with the physical injuries, I cannot be optimistic in my prognosis." The physician did order her hair cut, lest the heavy tresses drain what energy the poor girl maintained, and he did bleed her, to relieve the swelling. "That's all I can do, Sir Malcolm. If she does not wake up on her own . . ." He shrugged. "Now we can only pray."

"Pray for the devil to claim his spawn," Sir Malcolm muttered as he sent the doctor on his way.

Sir Malcolm never did ride toward the inn. When the captain's note was delivered, he sent his wife to search the girl's room. She'd packed a valise; no one came and forced her to run off with a blackguard extortionist. He tore up the note. When the messenger came from the magistrate, babbling about how Captain Anders was dead, his daughter Lucinda responsible, Sir Malcolm replied, "I have no daughter." And when they brought her battered, frozen body home, he almost had them deliver her to the poorhouse or the church or the livery stable, he cared not which. Only his wife's whispered "What will the neighbors think?" kept him from slamming the door on the poor fool of a magistrate who'd spent hours searching the countryside for the jade.

Lady Edwina looked at her husband across her daughter's still form in the big bed. "No one will have her now, not even Halbersham."

"No matter, you heard the doctor. If she hasn't woken by now, she likely won't. If the fever does not carry her off, she'll waste away unless someone spoons sustenance into her. Likely a futile effort anyway," he said. Sir Malcolm glared over at Lucinda's old nanny. "So we need not try too hard. Is that clear?"

Lady Edwina wrung her thin hands. "Oh, the shame of it all. There's no dressing this up in clean linen, not with half the county hearing about it already. What will I tell our friends?"

"Nothing. We simply won't receive anyone for the week or two this should take. Then we can go away."

They left the darkened room, discussing the merits of Jamaica versus Greece. Only Lucinda's old nanny stayed behind, weeping.

Chapter Two

$\mathcal{K}$ieren Somerfield, sixth and possibly last earl of Stanford, was a tidy person. He conscientiously wiped his Hessians on a faded Turkey runner in the marbled hall of Stanford House, Grosvenor Square, and carefully draped his caped greatcoat over the back of a Queen Anne chair that was missing an arm. Sweeping the lamp left burning there for him in an arc, he made sure everything in the grand entry was in order: no valuable pictures on the wall, no ornate candle sconces, no Chinese urns filled with hothouse flowers. Kerry shrugged his broad shoulders. Poverty as usual. He made his way to the study at the rear of the house, one of the few rooms in the mansion currently in use.

'Twas easier to keep clean this way, more considerate of Demby, his man-of-all-jobs, few-of-them-by-choice. The earl owed his only servant so many months' back wages, Demby must be staying on for room and board. That and the scarcity of positions for a groom whose hands shook so badly he took half a day to tack up a horse, or a valet so palsied 'twould be a death sentence to ask him to shave you. The neckcloths Demby tied more likely ended under the earl's ear, and his cooking more often landed on the kitchen floor than on the table. The man had sworn off drink, though, and did manage to get Stanford's clothes pressed, his mail delivered, his bed made up, the stable mucked out, and his watch redeemed from the jeweler when the dibs were in tune.

The earl hadn't known the hour for some weeks now. It was obviously time to get his life in order.

In his study Kerry rekindled the fire, then gathered scraps of paper from his desk, his drawers, his pockets. Fastidious as ever, he made neat stacks of the letters and notes.

The first pile was for tradesmen's bills, complete with dunning notices for payments in arrears: the grocer, the vintner, his clubs, a coal dealer. A great percentage of these bills were from the finest tailors, bootmakers, and hatters in London. The earl was very particular in his dress, particularly for a man with pockets to let.

The next bundle was for debts of honor. He smoothed out the crumpled notes from his pocket and penciled in some figures on others. These were gaming debts, vowels, chits—fortunes owed to other members of the sporting class. Since inheriting his father's honors, along with the fifth earl's debts and mortgages, Kerry had made his living by his wits. They'd gone begging, too. His horses were like to trip at the gate, aces seemed to have a magnetic attraction to his opponents, and the dice could be round, for all the mains he hit. Hell, these days if he wagered the sun would rise on the morrow, likely the world would end today. But somebody would be around to collect, he was sure.

He got up to pour himself a brandy from the decanter left on the mantel. When he got back, the stack of vouchers on his desk looked even taller. Taller than his own six feet, taller than a mountain. Kerry swallowed down his glass and tried, unsuccessfully, to recall if there was any gudgeon on earth who owed him money.

The next batch of papers were all official-looking documents. The earl did not need to read the letters from his bank enumerating his mortgages or the interest payments due. The bank wrote to him often enough that he had the figures memorized. As for his account balance, well, the bank did not waste postage when there was nothing to report. Downy birds, those banking fellows, his lordship thought, pouring another glassful. They watched every last groat.

The final pile consisted of letters, which took another brandy to open and read. His steward at his seat in Wiltshire reported two more of the few remaining tenants—and their rents—moved off to better-yielding lands, half the fall harvest lost to flooding, and the roof of Stanford Abbey itself about to collapse.

The dowager Lady Stanford, Kerry's loving mother, wrote a brief, affectionate letter in which she fondly recalled that Kerry's properties were in disrepair, the earldom was in danger of extinction, and his way of life was not conducive to a doting mama's mental well-being, but she was, as always, contributing what assistance she could. Of course, those were not the exact words she used. Hers were more like *gudgeon*, *popinjay*, and *wastrel*, with demands he marry an heiress posthaste, before she was forced to pawn her last piece of jewelry just to keep a roof over her aching head. And, by the way, she'd concluded, all of the housemaids had left because Aunt Clara was talking to Uncle Nigel again.

Uncle Nigel, his father's younger brother, had gone overboard on a fishing expedition when Kerry was barely seven, some twenty years ago. Aunt Clara was positive Nigel's spirit haunted Stanford Abbey, waiting for her to join him in the Great Beyond. As expected, Aunt Clara's letter was full of Uncle Nigel's advice and pronouncements: Nigel

14

thinks the roof tiles can be repaired, Nigel thinks the south quarter fields can be drained into a ditch across the home woods. If Uncle Nigel knew so much, Kerry wondered, how come he never learned to swim? And why the deuce did he have to leave his widow without a feather to fly with? In Kerry's poor, dilapidated nest, no less.

Aunt Clara's final remark, that his mother was keeping company with a smuggler, he ignored. The Countess of Stanford and a personage called Goldy Flint? Even Kerry's befuddled mind rebelled at that notion. The woman was as queer as Dick's hatband, that was all. The two widows cordially loathed each other, giving Kerry another excuse to avoid visits to the ancestral pile, if overwhelming debts and impossible demands were not enough.

The papers were all neatly arranged, corner to corner across the desk. On the top of the piles of bills and notices the earl placed his assets: the last bottle of brandy, a handful of coins from his pocket, and some lint. He opened the bottom drawer of the desk. He had no way of repaying his debts, no stake to make another wager, nothing to send to keep the abbey from crumbling into dust. No heir, no hope. He did have his father's prized dueling pistols. Kerry tenderly placed one of the silver-sided Mantons in the exact center of the desk.

"Drat. He said this task was hard, not impossible."

"Demby? Is that you, man?" The Earl of Stanford squinted into the shadows at the other end of the room.

"And I should have known better than to believe that devil. There isn't a male anywhere a girl can trust, living or dead."

"Demby, if you've brought one of your dollymops into my study, I'll—" Kerry's words were cut off by a cough as his nose and throat were assailed by an awful stench. "Gads, something must have died in the chimney. I wonder if the sweeps will come on credit," he muttered as he went to open a window. The smell of rotten eggs and boiling tar abated somewhat, mingling with London's usual rank odors. He took a deep breath of the cold night air to clear his eyes and his lungs—and his head.

"That's right, enjoy the cold now; it's the last you'll know for a long, long while if I can't do my job."

Kerry spun around. There *was* a woman in the room, and what a woman. This wasn't one of Demby's barmaids either, not if he was any judge of the demimondaine. This luscious creature had to be one of the highest-flying birds of paradise on three continents. She was small, but shaped like a goddess, with flame-colored hair trailing down her back. The shimmering red-gold gown she wore was so sheer, he could see the nipples painted to match her lips and her nails and her toes. Gads, the brazen baggage was barefoot. Kerry licked his suddenly dry lips. "I am sorry, *chérie*—you'll never know how sorry—but I just cannot afford your services tonight. I do admire your, ah, initiative, though."

"Afford my . . . ?" She gasped, which served to lower the neckline of her gown into near nonexistence. "You think I'm a . . . Oh, my, I'll *never* succeed."

"*Au contraire*, my dear, I think you'll be a bigger success than Little Harry. You could have every buck in London at your feet in a sennight, if that's your goal."

"Well, it isn't. My assignment is to lead you to the path of righteousness!"

Kerry laughed till tears came to his eyes. "Congratulations, my dear. That's the cleverest remark I've ever heard come out of a whore's mouth."

"I am not a . . . what you said, and this is not a laughing matter, my lord. Your whole life, for all eternity, could be decided tonight, and mine along with it. I just *have* to get you to renounce your life of sin."

"You? Ma'am, I beg to tell you, you make a very unlikely evangelical. Why, you could lead the Archbishop of Canterbury straight to hell with one blink of those incredible green eyes."

"Me? Drab little Lucinda Faire?"

"Fishing for compliments, are you? Drab? Have you looked at yourself recently?"

"Well, no. You see, I have this problem with mirrors. I can tell, however, that this dress is like nothing I've ever owned." She ran her hands along the silky material over her thighs. His lordship didn't breathe again until she murmured, "It feels rather nice."

Rather nice? Kerry swallowed, hard.

Lucinda was twirling one of those fiery curls in her hand. "And I am sure my hair was never so red, just a streaky kind of blond. And it never took a curl like this. It must be the heat."

His lordship was fairly overheated himself, watching her. Before he grew too uncomfortable, he tried to get her to leave again. "This has been pleasant, miss, a truly novel approach, but I really have other business tonight, as I am sure you must also. If you would just come this way . . ."

Instead of following him toward the door, the female seemed to drift toward his desk. Her hand reached out for his pistol. "I killed a man, you know."

By Zeus, she was a Bedlamite! What a shame, for such a beauty. She must be someone's mad relative escaped from confinement. Zounds, he didn't want to send her into hysterics by shouting for Demby. He didn't want to end up shot either. "Miss, please, come away from there. That's a very delicate mechanism."

"Will you listen?"

"Yes, yes, anything."

Lucinda stepped away from the desk, but floated

gracefully out of his reach. "I did kill a man, truly," she began, and started to tell Lord Stanford about how her parents were very strict, and how they had arranged her marriage to a crotchety old man.

"I'm sure they meant well," he said, trying to hurry the tale along and not believing a word of it, or this whole bizarre occurrence. "The road to hell, you know. Paved with good intentions."

"No, it's not. It's paved with rakes and libertines, reaching and grabbing and slobbering over you." Then she told him about Captain Anders and the elopement with a sadness in her voice he couldn't help wishing gone. When she got to the part of how Anders confessed it was all a pack of lies to get her father's money, and how he wanted to ruin her to complete the plot, Kerry found himself wishing the bounder were still alive, so he could shoot him.

An actress, that's what she was, he decided, gathering his thoughts again, an incredible actress who almost had him believing that farrago of nonsense. She'd gone from seductress to lunatic to innocent child in a matter of moments. One of his friends must have hired her for his entertainment. Kerry smiled at the thought of what kind of entertainment was in store, if she was as talented in bed as she was in the drawing room. Then her words drew him back.

"So I hit my head. Now, for all intents and purposes, my father's especially, I am dead."

"Dead? You mean you're a ghost?" Actress, he'd believe, prostitute definitely, but this was too much. She was back to being dicked in the nob.

"No, not exactly a ghost, since I'm not precisely dead yet. You see, things have been fairly slow at the Gates these days, what with the peace talks and the new smallpox inoculation, so they decided to hear my case before the fact, as it were."

"They?" Kerry had heard one should always humor a madman. "What happened to St. Peter?"

"Oh, he took the pleasant job of welcoming new

arrivals. He leaves the messy details of deciding who goes where for the women to handle. Typical male, don't you know."

Kerry's mouth was hanging open by now. He could only repeat: "The women?"

"Oh, yes, they run everything. Anyway, St. Joan was there, and St. Ermintrude, and that Queen Medea for the opposition. But they couldn't decide. I *did* disobey my parents, and I *did* cause Captain Anders's death, directly or not." She paused and looked down at the hands clasped in her lap. In a near whisper she confessed, "And I did know lust. I wanted him to kiss me, at first."

"A kiss? You call that lust? Why, every red-blooded female—"

"So I was destined for hell," Lucinda interrupted. "But I had led an exemplary life before then, and I was truly sorry Captain Anders was dead. I could not regret pushing him, of course, only the result of it. So the angels struck a bargain with the demonesses." She looked up and smiled, showing perfect dimples. "I can go to heaven if I save you from hell."

Chapter Three

"*H*ell and damnation!"

"Exactly, my lord." She was smiling now, pleased with his understanding.

"You mean you expect me to believe that a parcel of females, all martyrs and murderesses, got together and decided my fate?"

"And mine, my lord."

He ignored that. "You're saying that females run the show there? What about God? What's He doing while all this is going on?"

"He? I'm afraid you're not ready for all of this yet, my lord."

"But I am more than ready to be shut of this fustian nonsense. I really must ask you to leave, miss. I don't know how you got in—it's not like Demby to be so careless—and if someone paid you, tell him it was an excellent joke while it lasted. But let me give you some advice, ma'am, if you wish to continue your career, whichever career you choose. Do drop the missionary gobbledygook. You're liable to be labeled a reformer, and no one is comfortable around a moralizing zealot, especially any gentle-

man you'd like to encourage. No one takes that religion stuff seriously these days."

"Sad, isn't it?" Her tone was wistful, but she did
move toward the door in a graceful, gliding sort of
motion.

Relieved the female was finally taking his hint,
which was more an outright request, the earl
vowed he'd have Demby's head in the morning if he
found the man had let her in.

Lucinda paused at the sofa where she'd been sitting. She bent over to pick up her slippers, then
kept bending until her softly rounded derriere was
in the air, wiggling as she searched for something
else underneath the furniture. Kerry loosened his
cravat before he strangled. Damn, she was good.
Too bad she was queer in the attic, and too bad he
was punting on the River Tick. If the chimney
sweeps didn't take credit, bits of muslin never did!

"Oh, my," Lucinda exclaimed, blowing a dustball
back under the couch. "Haven't you ever heard
that cleanliness is next to godliness?" Still bending,
she wiped her hand along the length of one shapely
hip.

Kerry clenched his teeth, murmuring something
about the devil preaching gospel, and almost
reached out to thrust her forcibly from the room before he was tempted past endurance. Then he
caught the gleam of something under the sofa.
Along with another fluff of dust was a shiny yellow-
boy, two crumpled pound notes, and the diamond
stickpin he had thought lost in some boudoir or
other ages ago.

"By George, that's marvelous!" he exclaimed, re-
trieving the bounty as she stood. He rose and held
out one of the pound notes. "Here, you keep this,
for bringing such luck."

She shook her head. "Luck had nothing to do
with it, my lord. I told you, I'm here to—"

Kieren, Lord Stanford, that nonpareil among the
Corinthian set and paragon of fashion, was already

back on all fours, searching beneath the rest of the furniture. "Blast, only a silver button."

The woman was gone when he straightened up. Kerry shrugged. She had been a diverting interlude, no denying, but now he had business to attend to. Two pounds, a golden guinea, and a stickpin weren't much of a fortune, but they more than tripled his current holdings. He couldn't begin to pay off even the smallest of his obligations, but now he had a stake. Not much of one, for certain, but enough, with Lady Luck on his side. Or whoever that peculiar ladybird was.

His lordship went to bed for a short sleep, blessing Demby's careless housekeeping. His dreams may have been filled with scarlet women, but he still woke refreshed and eager. A bath, a change of clothes, some of Demby's wretched coffee with the grounds still floating in it, and he was ready. He left the two pound notes with his servant for safekeeping. "And do see about the chimneys, Demby, that odor was appalling."

Manton's shooting gallery was thin of custom so early in the morning, but there were enough sportsmen practicing their aim to offer a bit of competition.

"Shall we make a little wager on the results, gentlemen?" The earl was priming his father's silver-sided pistols.

"With what, Stanford? I'm still waiting on that monkey you owe me from last week at Crockford's." Lord Thurston curled his lip.

"The end of the month, dear fellow, the end of the month. No, I meant a friendly little bet, just to keep the practice session interesting. I say, that's a pretty little trinket you have in your neckcloth. Not an heirloom or anything, is it? No? Then care to chance it against my diamond?"

The earl couldn't lose, not today, not with his father's perfectly balanced pistols, a clear eye, and that lucky gold piece in his pocket. Soon he had a collection of stickpins, snuffboxes, and silver shoe buckles, a magpie's horde indeed. Kerry whistled all the way to Reyerson's, one of the lesser Bond Street jewelers.

Lucinda, meanwhile, was at the lending library doing research. Two matrons vowed to take their trade elsewhere, and one purple-turbaned dowager had to have feathers burnt under her nose, so bad was the smell. A rat must have died in the wainscoting, one of the harried clerks suggested as he reshelved books no one admitted to taking down. *Paradise Lost* and Dante's *Inferno* were not the usual fare for the ladies who came to Hookham's for the latest Minerva Press offerings.

Reyerson's was not as distinguished as Rundell and Bridges, but it was more discreet, catering to the bucks and bloods of the ton, rather than the beaus. The losers at Manton's would know where to go if they wished to ransom their trifles; that was the accepted thing, and Reyerson was accommodating. A fellow didn't run so much a chance of meeting his mother's correspondents while he redeemed his watch there, either.

Kerry had his watch, his diamond stickpin, and a purse that jingled cheerfully when he turned to leave the premises.

"By Jupiter, it's Stanford! Just the chap I was hoping to see!"

"You were? That is, delighted to see you, too, Fortnam. Been out of town, have you?" The earl's mind worked frantically, trying to recall his old friend's name on any of the betting slips he owed. "The end of the month—"

"Just in town for a day or two, don't you know, never believed I'd run into you like this. Congratulate me, man, I'm married."

Fortnam could have demanded the deed to

23

Stanford Abbey and Kerry would have been less surprised. "Leg-shackled, you? I never thought I'd see the day!"

"Yes, I know, more's the pity. I can't believe I waited so long. Kerry, it's the best thing that's ever happened to me."

They shook hands again. "Thrilled for you, Fortnam. Who's the lucky lady? Do I know her?"

"No, and you never shall if I have my way, not with your reputation with married women. She's from the provinces, never even had a come-out, never wants one, she says."

"A gem beyond price." The earl stared pointedly at the gaudy bracelet in his friend's hand. Fortnam's ruddy cheeks got redder.

"Not at all the thing for Frederica, of course. It's a parting gift for Mimi."

"What, never say you are giving up the delightful Mimi, and for a mere wife?"

Fortnam laughed. "Just you wait, my boy. It'll happen to you someday. But that reminds me why I was so glad to see you. Here." And he took out his checkbook and wrote a draft on his bank for a hundred pounds. "Remember that old wager we had over who would turn benedict first? I'm more than happy to pay up. No, don't argue. I know you're going to say to keep the money for a wedding gift, but I really want to settle up the best bet I ever lost."

Kerry was just staring at the note in his hand. A hundred pounds? "I don't know what to say. I—"

"That's all right, Stanford, I know you can't believe it's me touting parson's mousetrap, but you really ought to try it. Of course, my Frederica is divine. You ought to find an angel for yourself, man."

A hundred pounds? "I believe I may have met one just last night."

The stickpin money went to purchasing a pretty tea service for the newlyweds; half the hundred pounds went to Demby, for safekeeping.

"And I don't care what the blasted chimney sweep said, something's wrong with this fireplace that's stinking up the room. Call in another if you have to."

When he shut the window—demned waste, letting his coal heat all of London—that woman was there again. Her gown didn't seem quite as sheer, or quite so skimpy. Perhaps it was a trick of the daylight, for she certainly hadn't lost any of her allure. "My, you are persistent," he said, thinking of the fifty pounds in his pocket. He really needed it for the card game later, but . . . "What is the price, anyway?"

"To keep your soul from eternal damnation? They wouldn't give me specifics, so I've been trying to find out."

Kerry ran his fingers through his carefully arranged brown curls. "Persistence be damned. Not that moralizing tripe again, I pray you. Just name a figure."

"It's too bad you are not a Papist," Lucinda went on as if he had not spoken. "You could simply confess your sins, sincerely repenting them, of course, and be spared the hellfires."

The earl lit a cigarillo, a sure sign of his frustration, that he might smoke in front of a lady—no, a female, even—without asking permission. "Ma'am, you are sin personified, and I confess I am already burning for you. The only thing I might repent beyond the cost is having to listen to any more of this claptrap. Sincerely."

Lucinda stamped her foot. "Oh, how am I going to make you pay attention?"

Kerry inhaled deeply on the cigarillo. "I assure you, *chérie*, you have my complete and total attention." Then he watched as the lightskirt bit her lip in concentration, muttering words he thought sounded like *rattle-pated rake* and *bone-headed bounder*. This dasher was certainly adding new dimensions to the oldest profession.

25

He exhaled in a perfect ring. Lucinda's scowl turned into a smile as she waved her arm through the smoke without disturbing the circle. Kerry blinked. "Excellent, ma'am, although I did have more in mind than parlor tricks."

"Oh, you must have buckram wadding where your brain is supposed to be! I know, touch me."

"At last."

Now, a gentleman would have reached out in a gentle caress along her cheek, or a soft stroke on her bare upper arm. Stanford was well past the stage for gallantry. He reached to wrap his hand around one of those enticingly round, milk-white globes that were barely concealed by the bodice of her gown. And touched nothing. His fingers tingled, but there was nothing in them. Nothing.

Lucinda gasped and swung her arm back. Kerry didn't duck; he knew he deserved the slap. Her hand came around and he felt the air whoosh by, and that same tingle, but no contact. Nothing. Silently Kerry reached out again, this time gingerly, respectfully. He tried to touch her arm, tried to feel one of those silky red curls, even the fabric of her gown. Lucinda let him, standing still, and even reached toward him, as if to smooth away the frown lines between Kerry's eyes. The hair on the back of his neck rose, the way it did when he was out in a lightning storm, then he felt light-headed, as if he were about to faint. He sat down in a hurry.

"My God, I didn't know my imagination was that good!" was all he could say when he could speak again.

Lucinda nearly ground her teeth in aggravation. "It's not, you clunch. I am not a product of your muddled mind, not even a night dream. I found the diamond stickpin for you, remember?"

"Then you're a . . . ghost?"

"I told you, I'm not dead yet. I'm just between positions right now, somewhat like an unemployed governess."

"Not an angel?"

"And never like to be if you don't show a little more cooperation, my lord."

Kerry got up and poured himself a brandy. His hands were shaking worse than Demby's. Still, he managed to get most of the liquid down his throat before sinking back into his chair at the desk. Lucinda was sitting atop the cherrywood surface, swinging her bare feet.

"So you're a minion of the devil," he asked, "here to save my soul? I thought it was the other way round."

"Heaven knows the devil doesn't need any more souls. And I am not quite consigned to hell yet either, so they gave me the opportunity to save both of us."

"Uh, are you so sure I'm destined for Hades?"

"My lord, do lust, gluttony, vanity, and sloth mean anything to you?"

"I think you have just described the Prince Regent."

"Gambling? Gossiping?"

He was glad he'd thought to bring the bottle with him so he didn't have to get up again. He didn't bother pouring into a glass either. "And every other gentleman of fashion in London. It's not so bad."

"It's not so good. Can't you see, the tonnish life is leading you to perdition."

"Dash it, if I'm so wicked, then why did they even bother sending you? Assuming, of course, that any of this is real."

"They sent me because they thought there might be hope for you. Someone spoke on your behalf."

"Must be Uncle Nigel. He speaks to everyone. Well, I hope you can help with this mess." His hand indicated the bills and such still in neat piles on the desk in front of him.

"That's nothing compared to the mess your immortal soul is in."

The drink was taking effect. The earl flashed

Lucinda a sweet smile. "Then one more sin won't matter. What did you say your name was?"

She sat up straighter and stopped swinging her legs. "Miss Lucinda Faire, my lord."

"I'll never accept you as a prim and proper Miss Lucinda Faire. Why, if St. Peter ever got a glimpse of those ankles, he'd never let you out of the Pearly Gates."

Lucinda thought she blushed, but without a mirror, of course, she couldn't be sure. "I have already been taken in by two silver-tongued devils: the one who got me into this fix in the first place, and the one who set me the impossible task of reforming a confirmed hellraker. So don't waste the effort of turning me up sweet, my lord. You may call me Lucinda, Lord Stanford, since we are to be such close companions."

"And I am Kerry to my friends and fellow fiends, Lucinda. No, Lucy, that's better. Ah, Lucy Faire, how clever. Let's have another drink to toast the partnership."

"Demby, do you believe in ghosts? Angels, devils, any of those spirit things?"

The earl's loyal servant removed the decanter from Lord Stanford's limp fingers without spilling more than a drop, so low was the level of brandy remaining. "No, my lord," Demby grumbled on his way to fetch a pot of coffee, "but I do believe in the demon in the bottle."

Chapter Four

"I'll never touch another drop of liquor," Kerry swore, clutching his throbbing temples. Demby's hands, all four of them, were shaking worse than usual as he held out a tray with some noxious brew guaranteed to cure the earl, if it didn't kill him first. The motion of the tray was making Kerry seasick, and the rattling of the cup was hammering stakes through his eyeballs. "God, I need a drink," he groaned.

"No, my lord, you need a clear head for tonight. Remember?"

His lordship couldn't remember his name right then, only a recurring nightmare about the most beautiful woman who never existed. He shook his head, a definite mistake. When the walls stopped revolving, he grabbed for the cup before Demby sloshed the entire contents onto the carpet. "Tonight. Right, the game. I still have fifty pounds, don't I? And my lucky gold piece? Don't worry, Demby, we'll come around."

"We'd better, my lord."

* * *

A few recuperative hours later, Lord Stanford was on his way to hell. Gillespie's gaming hell, to be exact. He eschewed Whites and his other clubs, where too many members held his vouchers, and the exclusive gambling dens where the stakes were too high for his present circumstances. Gillespie's was perfect: respectable enough that he'd find enough gentlemen mixed in with the cardsharps and ivory-tuners, not so refined that every player was already a creditor.

The rooms were dingy, dark, and overheated. The smell of stale wine and stale bodies hung over the tables, mingling with clouds of smoke. Fevered eyes and feral smiles greeted the earl as he passed by the roulette wheels, the dicing tables. He wouldn't want to spend eternity here, Kerry thought with a grin, but for tonight Gillespie's was ideal.

He played at vingt-et-un for half an hour or so, winning some, losing less. He did better at the hazard table, steadily increasing his rolls of house markers, wagering conservatively, and moving on as soon as his luck shifted. The roulette tables never interested him before, but this evening he placed a rouleau on red. And won, doubling his bet. He left both wager and winnings on red, and won again. And a third time.

The other gamesters were quiet, waiting to see what he did. The croupier was watching with raised eyebrows. Kerry started to move his stacks of markers over to the black box, when he chanced to look up. "Lucy?"

"Milord?" the dealer was ready to spin. Lucy was shaking her head. He left the chips where they were.

"Lucky, I meant to say. Red has been lucky for me."

"Number twenty-seven, odd, red."

Dazed, Lord Stanford gathered his considerable take onto a tray a waiter provided and followed Lucy into the shadows. She was in that same carmine gown that could have been painted on her. For some reason he found himself standing in front of her, shielding the view from the sight of the hardened libertines at the tables.

"What the bloody hell are you doing here?" he demanded in a harsh whisper.

"You could at least mind your tongue in front of a lady," she replied, not even looking at him but gazing over his shoulder around the room in wide-eyed innocence.

"This is no place for a lady!"

"Nor a gentleman with hopes of salvation," she reminded him.

"My only hope is to win a fortune, which I cannot do with you here to distract me."

"Are they really enjoying themselves?" She waved one hand at the scowling gamblers hunched over the hazard table. Kerry refused to see that her hand passed through his shoulder, leaving a slight vibration.

"Yes, and I would be, too, if you'd just go spread the gospel to some other poor soul." He turned his back and purposefully strode into Gillespie's second parlor, where smaller groups of men were gathered at card tables. Kerry sat at the faro table, determined to ignore what he didn't like. His concentration was off though, and he lost. Faro was too much a game of chance anyway. He stood and looked around and, right on time, spotted Lord Malverne, his quarry.

Malverne was well-to-pass, a heavy gambler, and none too needle-witted, by all accounts, although he won with enough frequency to keep him coming back. Sitting with him were two younger men, green but eager to lose the tidy bundles in front of them. No need to worry about taking vowels at this table. Kerry asked if he could sit in, and the youngest of the players, Wilson-Todd's cub, Kerry thought, nodded eagerly.

The other youngster dropped out shortly, the

stakes quickly growing too high for his resources, and his seat was taken by a cit with mended cuffs. He did not last long, nor the sideburned lieutenant who went down heavily for three hands, nor the grinning sot who wagered his whole roll on one hand, and lost. Young Wilson-Todd, Chas he called himself, was holding his own, while Kerry and Malverne were steady winners. Bystanders started to gather in a circle around the table, making side bets, some of which Kerry covered, extending his own winnings.

At a pause for a new player to take his seat and a fresh deck to be opened, Kerry took a sip of the excellent sherry at his elbow. He choked on it. Across from him, right behind Malverne, stood the flame-haired Lucy.

"Go away!" he shouted.

The tulip about to take up his hand rose in his seat. "I say, if you feel that way—"

"I told you, women do not belong here!"

The foppish gentleman in his yellow cossack trousers started to sputter. "I say, are you insultin' my manhood, sir?"

Kerry noticed him for the first time. "Who in tarnation is talking to you? Sit down and mind your own business!"

The dandy gulped, Adam's apple bobbing, but he stayed in his seat as directed. Malverne looked to Wilson-Todd, shrugged, and commenced the deal.

No one was staring at Lucy. Kerry couldn't believe it. He watched all the faces, those checking their cards, those making bets behind the chairs. Not a single slobbering smile was fixed on her half-naked chest, not one ogling eyeball was admiring her silk-draped legs.

"Your bet, Stanford."

They didn't see her, ergo she didn't exist. Kerry dragged his eyes away from the creamy white skin of her shoulders and concentrated on his cards. *He* didn't see her, therefore she didn't exist. Then why was the tobacco smoke taking on a burning pitch odor?

He lost that hand badly, and the next, trying not to consider the odds of red coming up four times in a row on a roulette wheel. Tarnation, he had to get himself in hand. He couldn't afford to lose from lack of concentration. By all that was holy, he couldn't afford to lose, period.

The next rounds went better as the deal progressed around the table, other players taking hands in the game, the bets getting larger, the pots in the center growing. Chatter died down as the ante rose. Wilson-Todd mopped the sweat beading on his forehead, another chap turned his jacket inside out for better luck, and a third player believed that serious gaming demanded serious drinking. He was seeking inspiration in a bottle of Blue Ruin. Malverne kept fussing with the lace at his collar, nervously picking at the picot at his shirt-sleeves. 'Twas his deal and his call. "Match."

"Raise."

"Fold."

"See your raise."

Kerry fingered the yellow-boy in his pocket and raised the bet again. So it went, in near silence, until only Malverne and Stanford were still playing for an enormous pot. Kerry's turn came again. His hand was good, not great. Pulling out of the game now would end his hopes for a big coup this night; staying in could cost him much of his holdings. Was Malverne bluffing? Kerry stared across the table, trying to look into the older man's eyes. What he saw was Lucy, leaning over the old roué's shoulders, her breasts practically spilling out of her gown into the dastard's lap.

"Hell and tarnation!"

"That's what I keep telling you, my lord."

Kerry looked around. They were all staring at *him*, not at her. Malverne was smiling. "Your call, Stanford."

The earl started to say "I—" but Lucy interrupted. "Did you know he has three aces?"

Kerry threw his cards down and jumped to his feet, his chair crashing to the floor behind him, drawing the attention of everyone in the room. He didn't care. "Blast it, that's cheating! You may think I am steeped in depravity, but I consider myself a gentleman and I will not play in a rigged game!"

At which Lord Malverne jumped up, threw down *his* hand—the three aces and two others which fell out of his sleeve—and ran out of the room before anyone knew what was happening or could stop him. Besides congratulations on his canny insight and gratitude for keeping them all from being gulled, Lord Stanford was also unanimously awarded the pot, and a considerable share of the cash Lord Malverne had left behind in his haste. That loose screw wouldn't dare show his face at Gillespie's to collect his booty, nor anywhere else in London, for that matter.

Kerry couldn't wait to get back to Stanford House to count his winnings. He even took a hansom cab, lest he be set upon by footpads. Once home, he made sure Demby was asleep, the rooms were all empty, the doors and windows all locked. Then he spread the gold, silver, and paper currency on his desk, ready to make his usual neat piles.

"They say 'tis easier to thread a camel through the eye of a needle than for a rich man to get into heaven."

Kerry groaned, then coughed at the fetid air. "Oh, no, not you again. You do not exist."

"Don't be any more foolish than you have to be, my lord. Am I not sitting right here in your leather chair?"

She was, right where there had been no one an instant before. He was sure the door was still locked; he was sure she was still the most exquisite creature a tired, overwrought mind could conjure up. If he could give her such kissable lips, he wondered, why, by all the saints, couldn't he get her to keep them closed?

"Of course I exist," Lucinda was repeating in some exasperation herself. "Well, for the next fortnight or so anyway. Which is not a great deal of time, after you have frittered away the last twenty-seven years. We absolutely have to come to some kind of accommodation here. Now, I've been taking notes." She pulled a sheet of paper out of the wall. Kerry sat down and poured a drink. Then he pushed it away and lit a cigarillo instead.

Lucinda wrinkled her nose. "Filthy habit, that. Anyway, the way I have reasoned it, we need some guidelines. I mean, you don't seem to see anything wrong with your way of life, and *they* don't see much right with it."

Lucy consulted her paper while the earl sat bemused. "I thought we'd start here, my lord. Do stop me if you recognize any of this. . . . 'I am the Lord thy God, thou shalt have no other God before me. Thou shalt have no graven images or bowing to other gods.' " She stared at the mounds of gold in front of Kerry, the coins he'd been idly trickling through his fingers. "So much for idolatry."

"God damn!" he protested.

" 'Do not take my name in vain.' Humph. 'Remember the sabbath day and keep it holy.' "

"I do. I went to church just a Sunday or two ago."

"That was a month ago, and you went only to collect the money Mortimer Greenstreet owed you. Then the two of you went to a prizefight. The next Sunday you stayed abed all day, still castaway from the evening before. The one after that you stayed abed with—"

"Enough! So I don't pay lip service to the mumbo jumbo they serve up in church."

"Hmm. 'Honor thy father and mother.' "

"Got you there," he said with a grin. "I wasn't the one who ran away from home."

35

"No, but you never *go* home."

"I am a good son," he blustered, although he couldn't keep from glancing to his mother's last letter right there on the top of the nuisance pile.

Lucinda had no need to read his correspondence. "The way you honor your father by caring for his ancestral property, begetting an heir to carry on his line? The way you listen to a lonely old woman's cries for your attention?"

"Ma'am, m'father was a basket scrambler of epic proportions. He ran the property into the ground and saddled me with more debts than I can repay in a lifetime. And m'mother's a fishwife."

"That's honor?" She went on before he could answer: 'Thou shalt not kill.'"

"Ah-ha! I never—"

"What about that duel with Sir Swindon? He died of your gunshot wound."

"He died of an infection, and he was a bounder anyway! He stole that opera dancer right out from under me, literally. And it was a fair fight. He had the choice of weapons."

Lucinda consulted her list again. "Strange, it doesn't mention opera dancers anywhere. Oh, here. 'Thou shalt not commit adultery.'"

There was silence at the other side of the desk.

"'Thou shalt not steal.'"

"There. I've never taken anything that didn't belong to me in my life, unless you're going back to some apples in the vicar's orchard when I was seven. You wouldn't hang a boy for that, would you, much less send him to hell?"

Lucinda gestured to the pile of tradesmen's bills, some of them years overdue. "What do you call that other than theft of services? How do you think the tailor and the baker feed *their* children? By letting them steal apples?"

His lordship had no answer. Lucy went on: " 'Nor bear false witness.' All that gossiping at White's can't be the truth. Even tucked away in Derby we heard how many a young deb's reputation was ruined by some careless bragging at the clubs. Are you going to tell me you never took part?"

"What, and bear false witness?" he asked impatiently. "What's next?"

" 'Thou shalt not covet thy neighbor's—' "

"Uh-oh."

" 'Wife, nor his house nor his fields.' "

"Well, there, I never coveted anyone's house or fields. Don't even see much good in my own acres, with farming such a dirty, unproductive business. And I can't help it if those old sticks keep marrying lasses twenty years younger than themselves." Kerry leaned back in his chair with his head cushioned on his crossed arms. "There, I didn't do so badly, did I?"

Lucinda did a quick tally. "Not only have you broken every one of the ten commandments, you've managed to justify your actions to yourself. You have no remorse." She sighed. "This is going to be a busy two weeks."

Chapter Five

"Demby, did you ever hallucinate? You know, see visions when you were in your cups?"

"Aye, my lord, all the time." Demby was holding out a fresh neckcloth. Kerry took it before the thing lost its starch from being fluttered about. "Great slimy monsters they were, too, slithery, snaky things, crawling all over."

"No gorgeous females?"

"Criminy, an' I saw gorgeous females, I'd still be drinking, begging your pardon, my lord."

Buckskin breeches molding his muscular legs, a coat of blue superfine stretched across his wide shoulders, and the neckcloth tied in a new knot, the windfall, the Earl of Stanford was ready to meet the day.

And a fine day it was, too. No clouds for once, no wind, and no interfering female, imaginary or otherwise. Kerry stepped jauntily out of the door of Stanford House. As usual, he did leave half of last night's winnings with Demby for safekeeping, but this time with instructions to put at least something on account on all of the tradesmen's bills, and to pay off the smallest and longest over-due.

Whistling, Lord Stanford was off to the races. A minor meeting was to be held at the oval near Warringdon, just outside Richmond. Lovely, brisk weather, superior horseflesh, convivial company—not even Lucy Faire could find fault with the day's entertainment.

Of course some of the races were fixed. Everyone knew the jockeys were frequently paid to lose apurpose, and often enough horses were nobbled, drugged or injured so they couldn't run the course. Still, it was the sport of kings, and a downy cove could win a king's ransom with judicious betting, inside tips, and a bit of luck. Kerry considered himself an excellent judge of horseflesh, he'd made friends with a paddock watchman, and his luck was definitely in.

The track was crowded, rough wagons alongside racing curricles, countrymen and clerks rubbing shoulders with turf rats and toffs.

Kerry found a boy to hold his horses, then made his way through the spectators, keeping a wary eye out for pickpockets and anyone who might wish to lighten his purse by demanding repayment of debts.

Lemuel, the guard, was holding fast to the gate, making sure no unauthorized persons had access to the horses. A few coins loosened his tongue.

"The rider of Aldebaran in the first was out here havin' a confab with Six Fingers O'Sullivan, then he went in passin' somethin' out among the other jockeys. An' in the second race, that Frenchy what trains Lord Finsterer's nags went 'round checkin' all the stalls, lookin' for some missin' tack." Lemuel placed his finger alongside his nose, and his other hand out.

Kerry filled the open palm and went off to place his wagers. He was careful not to put too much of the ready with any one bet taker, lest he change the odds on Aldebaran in the first or Lord Finsterer's Nightdancer in the second.

Aldebaran came in second. That threw off Kerry's parlaying calculations, but not by much. The day was still early. Then Nightdancer's jockey fell off partway through the last turn. His saddle slipped. Rumor around the track had it that Finsterer was too much a nipcheese to buy new leathers.

Kerry went back to Lemuel.

Lemuel scratched his head. "Well, in the third, that big gray do be the favorite on account of his trainin' times, but they ain't got him off to a good start yet. He don't like other horses next to or nigh him, so he'll balk at the gate."

The gray hated other horses near him so much that he finished ten lengths ahead of his nearest competitor. Kerry's long shot must have disliked the other runners, too; he stayed a long, long way behind them.

Lemuel whispered that Ruffles in the fourth had been given something to make him run faster; he was a sure thing. The only sure thing was that Ruffles dropped dead around the first bend, along with Kerry's hopes of amassing a fortune. He was losing too much on each bet and on Lemuel's misinformation, and there were only three races left.

"Blast, I'll pick my own losers."

He studied the horses, he studied the odds. He listened to track talk and carriage chatter, about this beast's sire, that gelding's last outing, a third one's rumored blind eye. Two minutes to start, and he hadn't placed a bet. "The devil take it," he swore.

And Lucy winked back at him across the track with a saucy smile. He rubbed his eyes. This was broad daylight and he hadn't had a drink all day. She could not be here. True, there were a few women scattered about, bachelor fare with escorts or looking for escorts. One or two ladies sat in their carriages, watching the races through opera glasses, well protected from the elements and the masses. No female ever strolled by herself through a race meet—hell, through the race track itself—daintily picking her way through the dirt and the droppings, twirling a red parasol over her shoulder. Lucy did, the sun shining gold in her red curls, and a matching ostrich plume curling along her right cheek. She winked at him again.

Lud, he was losing his mind.

"Last bets, gentlemen. Last bets."

He read the chalk board one more time. There at number five was a horse he hadn't noticed before, Devil's Handmaiden. He looked to the field, quickly scanning the numbers on the jockeys' backs. Number five was a smallish roan mare with the sun making golden glints on her red back. He put fifty pounds on her to win.

"But, gov, she's goin' off at thirty to one. That little filly don't stand a chance."

So he bet seventy-five pounds and put that oddsmaker out of business for the day. Kerry's winnings were enough to pay off a few more of his debts if he quit then, which, of course, he had no intention of doing.

He strolled down to the paddock to inspect the horses for the sixth race. Lemuel had a tip about the number seven horse, Riddles, how his name was really Faradiddle, a winner at last month's meet. "A few white-wash socks, a new name, and much better odds."

"What about that black gelding over there, number three?" Kerry wanted to know.

"Look at 'im, covered in sweat already. Nervous as a new bride. Why, that horse'll wear hisself out before the start. Now, Faradiddle outran 'em all a few weeks back."

Something about the black appealed to Kerry though, the small, intelligent head, the flowing muscles, the jockey's scarlet silks. He went back and consulted the betting boards. Number three's odds were ten to one. He placed a substantial sum on Riddles, or whatever the horse's name was today, to come in second. The bulk of his earlier winnings he placed with various bookmakers on number three, Impy, to win. Then he held his breath until the homestretch, where, unbelievably, Riddles and Impy were racing neck and neck. Impy took the lead, then Riddles. Lord Stanford screamed himself hoarse, almost willing the black to get his nose across the finish line first. Somebody must have been listening, for the black stretched his neck out just so, at just the last second.

The seventh and last race. Kerry was *that* close to having the wherewithal to pay off most of his debts; he could almost taste the freedom. But no horse looked promising and Lemuel had no tips. No names struck a chord. There was Bething's Folly, Minor Indiscretion, and Loyal Companion, but none seemed to speak to Kerry. Perhaps that was a sign he should take his winnings and go back to the baize tables. At least the cards required something beyond intuition or luck.

The earl was turning to make his way back to his curricle when he heard an angry shout from the crowd behind him. The favorite's name was being erased from the chalk boards and a new name was being entered in its stead, Salvation. Furious, the mob kept up their howl. No one had ever heard of the horse or even knew what it looked like. The jockey, Luke someone, was equally unknown, and the bookmakers couldn't begin to figure odds long enough.

No matter. Kerry smiled and put every last shilling on Salvation. And practically cried when the horse was led out of the paddock area and onto the track. Salvation was gray except for a white muzzle, sunken-chested, and stumbling. Why, it would be a miracle if Salvation managed to save himself from the glue pot for another day. He managed to amble to the starting line, facing in the wrong direction, while the other jockeys made jokes. Salvation's jockey appeared to be foxed, weaving around in the saddle and having trouble staying aboard. The crowd laughed, of course. None of them had any money on a superstitious, hallucinatory whim. Of course.

The jockey finally managed to get the ancient horse turned around and everyone settled down for the start of the race. No one else but Kerry seemed to notice that the scarlet-clad jockey had an ostrich feather in his cap. His? Kerry wasn't even surprised when Lucy smiled going around the nearest turn, dropping the reins and her whip—no, her parasol—to wave at him. His only surprise was that the officials didn't stop the race when she leaned forward to whisper in the horse's ear and the old nag started to fly toward the finish line. Literally. Oh, God. Kerry prayed for Salvation like no sinner ever had.

Half the money went to Demby for safekeeping as usual, after he paid off the rest of the household bills. With a celebratory bottle of champagne and a new stock of cigarillos, Lord Stanford joyfully prepared to pay his gambling debts.

"Fifty pounds to Cholly Spofford. . . . A monkey to Lord Cheyne. Devil a bit, I still think the match should have gone to the Dutchman. . . . Seventy-five for the curricle race I could have won but for that herd of cows . . ."

"Isn't it nice to know that now you can give up gaming?"

"Give up—Lucy?" The earl scanned the shadows of his study. There she was on the sofa, her feet tucked up beneath her. He thought for a moment what a charming domestic scene they made, he settling accounts and she at her embroidery. Except, of course, that he was paying gaming debts and she was dressed in a gown that could make a whore blush, and the room smelled of brimstone. And he was a rational, clear-thinking Englishman, and she didn't really exist.

"I'd kiss you for today's work, angel," he told her, "if you were real."

Lucinda knotted a thread and bit it off with her teeth. "Why are you so afraid to admit I exist?"

"Because if you exist, if you are who and what you say you are, I am crazy." Carrying his glass and the bottle, Kerry took a seat across from her near the fire, where he could drink in her incredible beauty.

"You'd rather consider yourself insane than headed for hell?"

He was watching her graceful fingers dart in and out of the fabric, rather than listening to her words. "What's that you're working on?"

"An altar cloth. The devil makes work for idle hands."

He laughed. "You? A painted harlot sewing on an altar cloth?"

"Why not?" she asked with a scowl. "*You* aren't aiding my cause any. And I do wish you'd get it out of your mind that I am a fallen woman. I mean, fallen from grace is one thing, but fallen off the primrose path is quite another. I strayed only that once, you know. Before that I was strictly trained in all the genteel arts like music and sewing and watercolors. I'll have you know that before meeting you I'd never been to a horse race or a card party."

Staring at shoulders that were almost bare except for two ribbons and a lock of hair, he sneered. "Somehow I cannot feel responsible for corrupting an innocent."

"I do realize from your, ah, admiration that I do not appear the proper young lady right now. No man has ever looked at me that way before, not even Captain Anders. While such, ah, attention cannot help but gratify my vanity, this"—she indicated her body, her clothes—"is merely the devil's handiwork. I do not intend to spend eternity looking like a doxy."

With that businesslike pronouncement, the needlework vanished and a piece of paper appeared in her hand. "How do you feel about 'God, King, and Country'?"

"Pardon me?"

" 'God, King, and Country.' You know, what the crusaders shouted before battles. I still believe we need some kind of credo, a workable system to get you into heaven. It worked for all those feudal types."

"It did? I mean, they were bloody-minded bastards. I'll thank you not to put me in any clanking armor for all eternity. I'm no blasted fanatic, b'God. And as for the king, the man is a hopeless lunatic. Everyone knows that. Would dancing with him on the parapets in my nightshirt show my moral fiber?"

"And country?"

"They wouldn't let me join up, blister it. The heir and all that, last in the line. I would have gone," he said, raising his chin.

"But you could have served your country by taking your seat in Parliament, and you never did."

"What, argue endless politics with those old bagwigs?" He had another sip of the champagne, then put the glass down. "I'm sorry, I never thought. Would you care for some champagne? I could fetch another glass if you'd prefer."

"I've never tasted champagne," she answered with a hint of regret. "But even if it were possible, the last thing I need is another vice."

"What, a tiny sip of wine? That cannot be so great a sin. And while we're talking about that, I don't see why I cannot go on as I have been, sowing my wild oats like every other buck in town. Soon enough I'll have to settle down, set up my nursery, take my seat, be an upright citizen. That's the natural way of things. Even m'father got religion before he died."

"Haven't you been listening? You might have another forty or fifty years to balance out your current dissolution, but I need you reformed now, in the two weeks or so before I die."

"You're wrong, you know. I have listened to you. I just haven't believed all the fustian. The doctor thought you could wake up anytime if you really wanted to. So why give yourself two weeks? You could have the same thirty or forty years to embroider altar cloths. That's a better bet than putting your money on me. Besides, there's champagne and waltzing. I wager you've never waltzed either. Why die if you don't have to?"

"There is no reason for me to live. I'd have no family, no friends, no resources, not even any references to get a position. Those pleasures you speak of are for the privileged, not destitute females with no reputations. Once my father casts me out, I'd have to become what you think I am, or starve. I'd rather die. Especially if I have hopes for a better life after, with your help, thank you."

"I still don't understand. If you are here to win me over to the side of the angels, why in hell are you in the guise of the devil's daughter?"

"It's because of the odds against my succeeding. Now, there's something in your ken."

"They gamble in heaven? Hallelujah."

"Of course not, silly. But purgatory has a special place for gamblers where they win all the time, so there's no pleasure in it."

"So the odds against my reforming are not good?"

"You've heard of a snowball in hell? So won't you please try?"

"Certainly, as soon as I see my tailor."

"Tailor!" she cried, clenching her fists. Of all the uncooperative, disaccomodating fribbles. "With all those bills and closets full of frippery waistcoats and such? I'm going to hell in two weeks and you're going to the tailor?"

"Certes, my dear, I need to be fitted for a strait-jacket."

Chapter Six

*A*fter spending the evening tracking down one creditor after another through all the clubs and gambling parlors of London, Lord Stanford sank into a contented sleep. A few hours later, unhappily, he awoke to an embarrassing dampness in his sheets for the first time in years.

A woman. He needed a woman, was all. Once the stress and strain of all those debts was lifted from his mind, his body had reasserted its own needs. He hadn't kept a regular mistress since Claudine, last year, and hadn't even partaken of the offerings of widows or wandering wives in months. Even those free spirits expected a show of gratitude his finances did not permit. Hell, in the past weeks a hasty doorway coupling with a Haymarket whore was above his touch, if not beneath his dignity. *That's* why he was seeing visions of half-naked women all the time, awake and asleep. Relieved to have a satisfactory explanation, Kerry got up and pulled on his clothes.

Fortnam's Mimi might still be available and in need of consolation, he thought. But demireps like

Mimi expected to be treated like ladies. One didn't call without an appointment, especially at three in the morning. He could always go down to Covent Garden and pick up a streetwalker. They were out all night. But who knew what else he might pick up there?

So Lil's place it would be. The girls were clean, the sheets were fresh, and Lil's cellar was superb—not that he meant to overindulge. Never again, once he started hallucinating.

Lil gave him an effusive welcome. Of course she did, word having spread through town that the dashing young earl was flush in the pocket again. In fact, tonight's surge of business could be credited to his account, what with at least three or four of his former note-holders spreading his rhino at Lil's.

"And lucky money I heard, too. The best kind, my lord. May Lady Luck stay looking over your shoulder, dearie, as long as one of my girls is sitting on your lap!" And she cackled so loudly, the bruiser by the front door came charging into the parlor. Lil dismissed the bully with one beringed hand. "So what's your pleasure tonight, my lord? Being so late and all, a lot of the girls is already in bed. Asleep, that is." She laughed again. "They'd be more'n happy to have you wake 'em, I'm sure, if you don't see what you want down here."

Kerry was already looking over the sleepy-eyed girls in the gilt-and-fringe-decorated parlor. They looked tired and pale despite the painted smiles trying to win his attention. He chided himself for being disappointed. What did he expect at Lil's, some pink-cheeked charmer with dewy eyes?

"I was, uh, hoping for a redhead," he heard himself saying. "Young, but, ah . . ."

"Bosomy?" Lil didn't go into this business yesterday. "I have just the girl for you. She's new and eager to please. You go on up with our Sally here. I'll send Lucille along in just a minute or two."

Lucille? Kerry gave the maid Sally a coin, but

she couldn't tell him anything about the girl, she was that new. He hung his jacket over the back of the small room's only chair, then started pacing. Not even noticing the faded wallpaper or the patched quilt on the bed, he paced until the door opened, then shut behind his lady of the evening.

Lucille. She was eager, all right, eager to tear him apart with her long, blood-red fingernails. Kerry'd heard of someone being so mad they smoked; he used to think it was a figure of speech.

Putrid fumes and fiery sparks billowed out of Lucy's mouth, nose, and ears. Red flame glittered in her green eyes.

"Uh, jealous, my pet?" Kerry bluffed. "If I thought for a second you'd have—"

"How dare you?" she roared, sending roils of smoke toward the ceiling.

Kerry backed up across the little bedchamber until his knees hit the narrow bed. He sat down and edged as far as possible away from this raging fury. If he'd still had doubts about her story, he was a believer now.

"That's right, cower. Cringe, you puny lordling. Where is the arrogant cynicism now? If I don't exist, why are your knees shaking? If you conjured me up from the depths of your depraved mind, why can't you conjure me into your bed? Why?" she ranted. "I'll tell you why, you boil on the butt of humanity. Because I, Miss Lucinda Faire, late of Fairview Manor, Derby, currently teetering on the brink of the River Styx, am in charge here."

Lucy clamped a hand over her mouth, suddenly aghast at what she'd said. Whatever happened to meek and dutiful little Miss Lucinda? She didn't recognize herself in this body, this virago, this . . . this bordello. This last restored some of her indignation, especially since she could see her outburst had finally penetrated his lordship's social veneer.

"I have been very patient," she went on in a milder tone, "waiting for you to see the error of your ways. Realizing that you are only a product of your times, and a male besides, I forgave your pride and pigheadedness. I have tolerated your insobriety, even your blasphemy. And I actually abetted you in your gambling, thinking that was the quickest way to set your mind on higher matters. But whoring? Whoring I shall not tolerate!"

By now Lord Stanford deduced that he wasn't about to be smoked like a kipper. Lucy needed him alive and kicking bad habits. He mopped his brow. "I, ah, did thank you for your assistance at the racetrack, you know."

Lucy was not appeased. "You'd better cherish your appreciation, my lord, for that was the last time. From now on, you bet, you lose." She crossed her arms over her chest.

Even in these circumstances Kerry noticed her chest was particularly generous. He smiled. "Cut line, Lucy, I didn't always lose, even without your help."

"You will now."

Somehow he believed her, not that he wouldn't test her assertion at the first opportunity. "But if I am not to support myself by wagering, how do you propose I live? Does highway robbery suit your notions of morality any better than gambling?"

"Don't be goosish." Lucy was studying the room. Her nose wrinkled at the damp gray towel, the chipped basin and unmatched pitcher.

The earl stood up, trying not to be embarrassed in front of her at the dirt in the corners, the darned coverlet, and cracked mirror. This wasn't his house, after all, just because he visited. "Now who is being goosish? You must know *my* father wasn't any nabob, Miss Lucinda Faire of Fairview Manor. All he left me were debts and obligations."

"And your heritage. It's past time you took up the reins of your responsibilities, my lord."

"What, become a country squire?"

"There are worse things."

"Not for me there aren't. Oh, I enjoy the horses and the open spaces, but waking at cock's crow and riding all day pall after a while. Furthermore, in case there is something you didn't know about my personal life, Stanford Abbey needs a major investment of funds just to make the mortgages, much less a living. Needless to say, without gambling I have no chance to find that kind of gold."

"I do know you haven't yet tried hard work."

He gave her a smile. "You think gaming is easy? Besides, the abbey doesn't require another strong back, it requires a degree of expertise I haven't got."

"Then learn," she said in exasperation. "If you can understand the rules and percentages for all those silly card games, surely you can manage to figure out crop rotation and irrigation."

"My father never did."

"Is that what you want *your* son to say? Oh, bother." She seemed to be looking for something, searching for nonexistent pockets or a dangling reticule. Finally she pulled a piece of paper from the air above her head. "Ah-ha. The code of chivalry."

"Now you're the one with attics to let. What in blazes does the code of chivalry have to do with mangel-wurzels and milch cows?"

"See, you do know something about agriculture." Lucinda was studying her notes, biting her lower lip in a way that made Kerry wish she really were Lucille, his belle de nuit.

"Don't you even think it, sirrah," she said, reading either his mind or the bulge in his breeches. "And the code of chivalry is another doctrine of conduct, one it might behoove you to consider as a modus vivendi."

"What, more medieval dogma? Are you going to bring back chastity belts, too?"

"One or the other might have kept you out of such a place as this."

There was an unmistakable note of disdain in

Lucy's voice that robbed him of the last amorous thoughts, but not regrets for what might have been. "And what's so wrong with a house of accommodation? It's just a service like any other, buyers and sellers. No one is injured."

" 'Chivalry,' " she read, " 'a canon dedicated to the protection of the weak, defense of the innocent, reverence for the purity of women.' "

"Here? Weak, innocent, pure? Were you born under a cabbage leaf? Prostitution is a trade the girls pick, like becoming a seamstress, only with more chance of advancement."

Lucy shook her head sadly. "Wickedness must weaken your mind, too. Come with me." And she took his hand. That is, she made his hand tingle, so he followed her.

Lucy led him down the deserted hall, around a corner, and up a flight of uncarpeted stairs. Motioning for silence, she pushed open one of the doors there. By the light of the hall candle, Kerry could see a room no bigger than a closet really, with a pitched roof that made it impossible to stand in, filled wall to wall with a ragged mattress. Three girls slept under one thin blanket, tumbled together like kittens.

"The one on the end is Lucille," Lucy whispered, nudging him forward.

Feeling like some kind of voyeur, Kerry ducked his head and took two steps into the room. Yes, there was the red hair, only it seemed to be the dead color of henna dye rather than auburn or carroty or Lucy's vibrant gold-streaked red. They'd forgotten to dye the chit's eyebrows, which were still pale brown. But she was young; Lil hadn't misled him about that. Sixteen perhaps, unless it wasn't just the innocence of slumber making her seem a veritable babe.

"Fifteen," Lucy whispered, "and fresh from the country. The family's farm fell under the enclosures, her brothers went to the mines. Lucille knew a girl who had a position as a housemaid in London, so her mother sold her wedding ring for the girl's coach fare. Lil met the coach."

Kerry could still see the tear tracks down the girl's cheeks. "My God, I didn't know—" But of course he did. He'd heard the stories, even joked how the girls got younger every year. "What can I do?" he asked helplessly.

"For Lucille? Nothing." He put a gold coin under her pillow anyway, before backing out of the room. There was a small chance she'd find it before one of the other girls did, or Lil.

"But you can do much for all the rest of the Lucilles," Lucy was going on as she preceded him down the steps, then down the carpeted public stairway and out to the cold night air. "You can speak out in Parliament against child prostitution. You can see that legitimate employment agencies meet the coaches. You can convince your friends that prostitution is degrading and that celibacy is a virtue. You can—"

Kerry was stopped in his tracks. "Hold fast, Lucy. I thought I just had to be a better man, not perform miracles!"

Lucy laughed and took his hand, which was an eerie feeling, but nice once one got used to it. "I have great hopes for you, my lord."

His watch at Lil's being over, the burly doorman took himself off to the Three Feathers for a heavy wet.

"Bash any heads tonight, 'Arry? Toss any sots in the alley?"

"Nah, more's the pity. Quiet night."

"Any fancy toffs come by, then?"

"Yeah, the Earl Stanford what they was sayin' had such a run o' luck this week. Must be true. 'E didn't even bat an eye when Lil doubled the goin' rate. Even tossed me a coin just for offerin' to call a hackney for 'im. Said 'e'd rather walk though."

The Three Feathers was shortly an empty nest as every cutpurse and footpad in the neighborhood lit out after the easy mark.

Kerry was deep in thought when the first assailant struck. He never heard the villain creep up behind him with a club in his hand, and he never turned around when the scoundrel slipped on a patch of ice—the only patch of ice in London that night—and knocked himself to flinders.

The next attackers worked in a pair. Except that one of them pulled his knife too soon and nicked his mate, who gave him an elbow in the breadbasket, which started a melee that distracted the next set of thugs into betting on the outcome.

Kerry kept walking, thinking of injustice, poverty, and the fate of unprotected innocents. Chivalry, almost, except that he wanted a woman more than ever. He didn't notice how a streetlamp somehow got between him and a tossed rock, or how a slavering pit bull decided to claim the block behind him as its own territory.

He didn't see the rat as big as a house cat run over Dirty Sal's foot, causing her to drop her pistol. He did hear her screaming, however. With thoughts of damsels in distress that would have cheered Dirty Sal no end, he turned in time to see two men coming at him with cudgels.

Lucinda decided to let the earl handle this attack on his own. She'd heard somewhere that men liked to feel important. Still ashamed of her own emotional outburst and shocking display of raw power—a lady never indulged in such disgraceful exhibits—Lucy felt she owed the earl a sop to his pride. Besides, he did need an outlet for some of that masuline energy, for she was going to make him toe the line, come hell or high water. She only hoped the ruffians didn't damage the earl's handsome face.

Kerry fended off the assault without raising a sweat. He did skin the knuckles of his right hand on one lowlife's chin, and ripped the sleeve of his greatcoat tossing the other into the side of a building, blast it. He'd finally got the curst topcoat paid for. Demby was no good at repairs, and the earl had to thread the needle for him anyway. Maybe he should just take up tailoring, now that he was renouncing gambling. Or perhaps he could become a prizefighter. Heaven knew he'd need some thrills in his life if he was to give up wine, wenching, and wagering. What other excitement was there?

So he went home and burned the house down.

Chapter Seven

*H*e didn't mean to start the fire, of course. Kerry just lit his cigarillo and sprawled back in his comfortable chair to contemplate his dreary future. Thinking of ways to circumvent those strictures—he hadn't precisely given his word to abandon the life of a London gentleman; there had been no chance yet to see if he could win a wager—he remembered the smoke and sparks coming from Lucy. Gads, she was magnificent when she was angry. Of course, he'd do his best never to provoke her again, but wondered if such a passionate nature carried over to other situations. Those heaving breasts, the flushed cheeks ...

Of course she did have that freakish layer of prudery. The earl contemplated trying his hand at a little reform himself. After all, even a saint should experience a few of life's finer things before giving them up. Thinking of some of those finer things, he fell asleep.

When his head hit the armrest, Lord Stanford awakened enough to take himself upstairs to bed, where the dream continued. Oh, my, yes. There was

Lucy calling his name, desperately urging him to hurry. There was that tingle, a frisson, a warm quiver to his face, his bare chest where she was grabbing at him in her frenzy. And there was that wretched smoke. How the devil did anyone make love with their eyes streaming and their throats gasping for fresh air? He coughed and sat up, awake.

"Thank goodness! There's not a minute to spare! Now, hurry!"

The room was filled with smoke and a distraught Lucy, trying to tug at him. He didn't see any flames, but the heat was uncomfortable and the smoke was unbreatheable. Staggering to the window, he threw it open and took deep cleansing breaths.

"Hurry! The fire!"

Kerry didn't wait for another warning. He grabbed up his coat, his purse, some papers, and his boots before hurtling down the stairs. That's when he saw the flames coming from his study and traveling along the faded Aubusson down the hall. The dry-as-dust wainscoting was smoldering, the ancient paper was curling off the walls. He ran through the great hall toward the front doors, away from the flames and thick smoke, glad for once that the place was no longer filled with priceless treasures.

Outside he shouted "Fire! Fire!" to draw the attention of the watch, who ran off to alert the fire brigade. He drew on his boots and his greatcoat, stuffing the papers and such in his pockets, and thought of going back for his father's Mantons.

Lucy was fluttering around the earl, anxiously patting him to make sure he was intact. "No, no, you mustn't. The whole place could burst into flames at any minute!"

Kerry supposed she was right. Besides, now he could buy a new pair if he had to. "Oh, my God, Demby!"

Racing around the side of the house, Kerry tried the service door. It was locked, of course. He tore off for the kitchen entrance at the rear of the house, and didn't even bother trying the handle. He just stepped back, then kicked the door in with his booted foot. Lucy was already inside, on her way to the apartment Demby kept near the kitchen, what would have been the housekeeper's rooms. "Hurry!"

The smoke was as bad here as on the upper story, the fire having traveled down the bare wooden servants' stairs. Kerry took two deep inhalations before plunging into the fire cloud.

Demby was in his bed, not stirring at Kerry's shout. Not breathing at all, in fact. The earl lifted the smaller man from the bed, blankets and all, and over to the window. Blessing the ground floor, he shoved his valet-cum-housekeeper out the window onto the shrubbery, and leapt out after him, dragging Demby to a safer distance away from the house.

"Breathe, man, breathe," he urged the gray-skinned man, shaking Demby's thin shoulders in a futile effort to jolt air into the man's lungs.

"The kiss of life," Lucy directed. "Give him the kiss of life!"

Kerry stared at her blankly. "The what?"

"Breathe into his mouth, you dolt! Hurry!"

The earl looked at his servant's unshaven face, straggly beard, stained mustache, and yellow teeth. "Like hell."

"Confound you for a gutless jackaninny, just do it."

So he did, and shook Demby again for good measure. Demby started to cough and wheeze and gasp for air, but he was breathing.

Lucy was radiant. "You did it," she cried, clapping her hands. "You saved his life! You endangered your own to save a fellow man, and then gave him your very breath! Oh, they have to appreciate this up there. Such a noble act has to cancel some of the wickedness, it just has to. So generous, so selfless, so—"

"So where's my stash?" Kerry thundered, shaking poor Demby again.

"Under the bed," Demby rasped. "With my collection."

Kerry dashed back into the house while Lucy shrieked like a banshee about his jeopardizing her chance for heaven with his recklessness and greed.

There were two boxes under the bed, so Kerry dropped both out the window before hurtling after, just as something in the kitchen exploded with a roar and a burst of new flames.

The fire brigade had arrived by then, in time to get a good view of the flames while their captain dickered with Demby over his lordship's lapsed fire protection policy.

Kerry opened his purse into the captain's hand. A new policy was instantly in effect.

"Exceptin' your lordship might also be interested in a benefit lottery we be holdin'. For the widows and young'uns of us brave firefighters, don't you know, what has fallen in the line of duty. Drawin's soon, and we only be sellin' a fixed number of tickets, so chances are pretty good."

"Better than the chances of any of your brave boys putting out my fire if I don't take a ticket, I suppose," the earl muttered, emptying his purse into the waiting palm. The captain whistled his men to work.

Demby was sitting up against the garden gate, blankets still draped over his shoulders. He was staring into one of the boxes, his stricken face looking more ghastly than it did when he wasn't breathing.

"Not the money, man, tell me the money is safe!" Kerry begged, falling to his knees next to the servant.

"No, my lord, your property is secure." He indicated the other box, where a household account ledger rested atop a leather pouch. "It's my, ah, collection."

"Deuce take it, I'm sorry if anything got damaged when I threw the box from the window. Didn't seem much choice at the time, you know."

"Of course not, my lord. And I believe the damage was done by the heat, not the fall." He held the box out with hands that shook less than usual.

Kerry looked in, then stirred the contents with one finger. "Uh, you were collecting candle stubs? I mean, I know it's been bellows to mend for a bit, but candle stubs?"

"Not candle stubs, my lord, wax carvings. Figurines I was going to have cast in bronze when we were in the chips again. Pewter, anyway. Here." And he unwrapped a piece of flannel to reveal a brass dragon small enough to fit in the earl's hand.

"Why, this is exquisite. Too bad it's not jade or ivory. Wherever did you come by such a fine piece of workmanship?"

"I had it cast the last time the dibs were in tune, you recall, when we did so well at Newmarket last year."

"You mean this is from one of the candle stubs? Uh, wax carvings? You're saying you did this? With a knife?"

"A chisel, actually."

"With your palsy?"

Demby took the statuette back with hands that didn't tremble at all. He coughed, as if there were still a residue of smoke in his chest. "The tremors passed when I stopped drinking, which is what cost me my apprentice mason job in the first place. I didn't like being a valet, my lord. Or a groom, or a cook, butler, footman, whatever. While you believed me incapable of performing all those duties, I had more time for my carving."

"Blast it, I hired you as a man-of-all-work," Stanford complained.

"But you never paid me, my lord."

What could the earl say? For one of the first times in his life he said he was sorry. "And for your collection melting. Lord only knows how, but I'll make it up some way."

"You already did, my lord, you saved my life. Besides, while I was lying there more dead than alive, an angel came and told me we'll come about."

"She wasn't wearing a red dress, by any chance, was she?"

"You know, I wondered about that very same thing."

Kerry sent Demby off to a hotel while he in his shirt-sleeves went to help the firefighters, carrying buckets and hoses. He even went with them to have a mulled ale after, to warm up. Just one. The captain said it was too soon and too dark to assess the destruction, but guessed it likely that the worst damage was from the smoke and water. The fire hadn't really spread yet, so the structure should be sound. Of course, it would take most of Kerry's remaining funds just to get the place clean and livable again, to say nothing of his clothes, household necessities, and buying the firemen a few more rounds.

He decided to bed down in the stables for the night rather than follow Demby to the hotel, thinking to guard against any looters bacon-brained enough to believe there was anything of value left in Stanford House.

He was counting the money Demby had been keeping, adding in the remnants from his purse and his pockets. He added the fireman's benevolent lottery ticket to the pile.

"You won't win, you know." Lucinda was sitting on an overturned bucket in the corner of the empty stall his lordship had selected as the evening's bedchamber.

She looked younger somehow, or perhaps the lantern glow made her hair seem more gold, less red. The sight of her still took his breath away, and not just because she'd appeared out of nowhere. "How can you be sure?" he asked.

"I just saved your life. Can't you trust me?"

"I never got a chance to thank you for that either. The firemen said it was a miracle the smoke didn't kill me."

"There's no need to look so humble." Lucy thought Lord Stanford was looking even more handsome than ever, in fact, brown curls all tousled and a smudge on one cheek. No wonder the man found it so easy being a rake. "I cannot very well save your soul without saving your life. Speaking of souls, no one has yet gone to heaven on a wager, so you may as well give poor Demby that raffle ticket to get his mind off his loss. We have nobler considerations."

"We do?" Still, he put the printed ticket away in the box, then shuddered as Lucy produced a thick sheaf of papers. "By Jupiter, ma'am, you don't intend to start reading me sermons, do you?"

"Would they do any good? I have it on high authority that you never paid proper attention to one before, so I misdoubt you'd start at this late date. I had thought to find defense of sorts for your behavior here." She tapped the papers. "The British legal code. Such things usually hold little sway with my, ah, superiors, but I thought if we proved you a model citizen . . ."

"That's the ticket. You can tell the lady judges I'm a regular upright law-abider. Never boxed a charley, never cried 'Fire!' in a public place, except tonight of course."

"Hmm. Do you know they have laws here in London about herding cattle through the streets, laws about crossing sweeps and sidewalk vendors and where Gypsies may camp? I'm afraid there is also a law about making duels illegal."

"The magistrate wrote it up as a hunting accident."

"And they did pass the Seditions Act."

"What, should I go to jail for saying the king is insane?"

"You did tell Lord Sidmouth that we were losing the war due to inefficiency, and you have mentioned that England would be better off with a few more bordellos than with any of Prinny's pavilion schemes."

"A man's entitled to his opinion."

"Not according to this law, he's not. But no matter." She sighed and tossed the papers into the hereafter. "The laws are very clear about arson."

"Arson? I never—"

"Your cigarillo did when you fell asleep and dropped it under the chair. Willful negligence. Leading to loss of property and endangering lives."

"I see what you're about. You're trying to get me to swear off tobacco."

"It's a filthy habit. See where it's led? And just think what would happen if Demby had died. The entire hallelujah choir couldn't keep you from hell."

The earl did not have any of his cigarillos with him, so it was an easy promise to make, but then he recalled that fiercesome display Lucy had put on at Lil's. Not above a little bargaining himself, he offered, "I'll stop smoking if you will."

Lucinda blushed. "I am truly sorry for enacting such a scene. I'm . . . just not myself these days. Yes, I'll agree to that. Shall we shake hands on it?"

The feeling of warmth traveled right up Kerry's arm to bring a smile to his face. "You know, you look different. Your hair, your dress. Something."

"Yes, isn't it wonderful?" Lucinda grinned back. "I even have a petticoat!" She clapped her hands to her mouth at the indiscretion. "Oh, dear, I shouldn't have said that. But I couldn't help feeling my attire wasn't at all the thing. But now . . . It's the odds, you know."

"The odds?"

"Yes, your chances of getting to heaven! You saved Demby's life and I got an undergarment!"

And a softer face, an inch higher décolletage, and satin slippers instead of decadent Roman sandals. Kerry sighed. Now he couldn't see the outline of her legs through the sheer gown. This business of reforming wasn't all a bed of roses.

Chapter Eight

*S*tanford House was salvageable, just. The stairs were unsafe, the parquet floors were buckled from the fire brigade's enthusiastic application of water, the wood paneling was soot-blackened, and the plaster ceilings were cracked from the heat and in danger of collapsing. On the other hand, the engineer reported cheerily, this was a fine opportunity to repair the dry rot on the upper story, the ill-fitting casements, and the antiquated kitchen.

Twitching in Lord Stanford's hands, not so cheerily, was an urge to strangle the fellow. The mandatory renovations alone would swallow his last shilling, leaving him with an unfurnished mansion, a fire-sale wardrobe, Demby, dry rot, and empty pockets. His watch and diamond stickpin might bring enough for new draperies, so the neighbors couldn't look in and see the Earl of Stanford sitting naked on the floor.

There was less than no chance of his borrowing another fortune either, with no unmortgaged collateral to put up, no future income to pledge away.

Deuce take it, he'd gone only one whole day without being in debt, besides.

Then again, he could just board up Stanford House and move to a hotel until his money ran out. Afterward he could batten on his friends, going from house party to hunting box as many of the ton did. Kieren Somerfield, hanger-on, left a sour taste in his mouth.

Blast, he was in as bad a case as ever, only colder. Sitting in the remains of his study with the windows open, Kerry huddled in his greatcoat, wishing for a drink. The last of his wine had been rescued by the fire brigade—liberated, more like it—and the kitchen was in no condition to produce even hot coffee. 'Twould take a squad of hardworking lackeys weeks to restore the kitchen to its former disreputable condition. Months, if they were under Demby's direction.

Kerry took out his gold coin, his lucky coin—hah!—and tossed it in the air. Heads he went ahead with the repairs, tails he abandoned the old pile. The coin slipped out of his hands on the downward arc, however, and rolled into a pile of debris, his former cherrywood desk.

Botheration, he thought, getting down on his hands and knees in the wet muck. He couldn't afford to let a ha'penny get away, much less a guinea. He'd wager it was the last he'd see for some time. Wager? What was it the chit had said about him betting?

Kerry found the coin and tossed it to his other hand. "Heads," he called. The coin showed tails. "Heads" again. Tails again. He called "heads" seven times, and got the reverse seven times. So he called "tails," and heads came up.

"Now do you believe me," Lucinda asked crossly, "or are you going to sit on the filthy floor all day, playing, when there's so much else to be done?"

Kerry scrambled to his feet and brushed off his breeches as best he could. Lucinda was perched on the window ledge, her dainty feet dangling into the room. She wore no pelisse, not even a shawl over that silky red gown, but Kerry's temperature rose a few degrees just looking at her. "Did you expect me to start mopping the floors, ma'am?"

"I didn't expect you to sit around feeling sorry for yourself."

"God damn, I'm not—"

"And I thought we agreed that you would give up blasphemy?"

"*We* didn't agree to anything, if I recall. You made demands and threats; I listened, that's all."

"Of all the thick-skulled, stubborn mules ... I suppose some of us cannot rise in the face of adversity."

"And I suppose some of us expect too much from others. Riding to heaven on my shirttails, indeed! Well, ma'am, let me tell you, you'd better find another driver. I cannot go around saving people from burning buildings and I cannot be giving alms to the poor, because I am one of them. So good deeds just aren't going to pull your chestnuts out of the fire. As for the rest, you'd better stop right now trying to make me what I'm not, for it won't fadge. I am a gentleman and I live by a gentleman's code. That's always been enough for me, and it shall have to do for you, too. The lady patronesses of Almack's are satisfied; I expect those inquisitors of yours can't be higher sticklers."

Lucy smiled in delight. "Then there is such a thing after all! I searched everywhere and couldn't find any gentleman's code written out."

"What kind of peahen looks for honor in a book?"

"Perhaps one who hasn't found it in the gentlemen of her acquaintance. Could you explain it to me?"

Kerry leaned against a bookcase long since emptied of anything but racing journals and old newspapers. He thought a moment. "Well, a gentleman keeps his word. That's the most important thing, so you can trust a chap if he makes you a promise. Like an I.O.U. That's play and pay, debts of honor when you put your name to them. And you can't cheat, of course."

"Is the whole thing concerned with gambling, then? They won't be happy about that."

He crossed his arms over his chest. "Of course not. There are lots of finer points to it, like always being dressed appropriately to the occasion."

Lucinda's lip curled. "I'm sure they'll be impressed with that."

"And the things fathers teach their sons at an early age: never pick on anyone smaller than you; don't foul your nest."

"Don't . . . ?"

Kerry picked a bit of dirt off the sleeve of his coat. "Don't bring loose women home to your mother. In later years, don't introduce your wife and your mistress."

"My, those are finer points."

"Never strike a woman," he went on with gritted teeth, "no matter the provocation."

"That's it?" Lucinda asked in amazement. "You cannot cheat at cards, but it's all right if you cheat on your wife as long as you're dressed correctly and she's not looking? Oh, and if she complains, you mustn't hit her. No wonder there are so few of your type in heaven!"

"That's not all of it," he practically shouted. "Ladies must be shown respect at all times, even if they are shrewish, nagging fiends from hell."

"Ladies, as opposed to serving girls or opera dancers?"

"All females deserve a gentleman's courtesy, some just more than others."

"And virgins?" she asked curiously.

"Virgins are to be avoided like the plague. Their virtue's such a fragile thing, a gentleman can find himself honor-bound to make an offer if he sneezes in their direction. Like being here alone with you.

If you were a real girl, which you're not, thank goodness, your reputation would be so tarnished after being with a libertine like me, I'd have to marry you. That would be the only honorable thing to do."

"Is that why you never married? You never compromised a lady?"

"I stay out of parson's mousetrap out of choice, not because I haven't been forced into it. Blast, you are sounding like my mother. I thought we were talking of honor, not marriage."

"Oh, I thought you mentioned something about fathers and sons. I don't suppose honor has anything to do with carrying on the family lines and all that."

Kerry looked away. "A gentleman is expected to perpetuate his name, yes. But not until he's damned ready!"

A pencil appeared in Lucy's hand. She licked the point before setting it to paper. "Now, let me see. You did give your word not to smoke."

"We shook hands on it, yes."

"And wagering?"

"I'm not gudgeon enough to bet when I can't win. It's only for two weeks or so anyway, isn't it?"

"I don't think that's the spirit of the thing. I'll mark that one with a question. Drinking?"

"To excess? I can't afford to. Besides, I got deathly ill last time."

"And you will next time, too." She left a blank and went on. "Cursing?"

"Damn—dash it, I'll try if it will end your nattering on about it."

"So I have your word on that?"

"To try, yes. I can't swear to minding my tongue every blo—blessed minute, but I'll try."

"And women." She made a big check next to that entry.

"Now, hold line, Lucy. You're the one who laid down the law there. I never promised any such thing. I mean, a female devil breathing smoke down a fellow's back can put paid to his desire. And if you're going to pop up anytime I feel randy and find myself a willing partner, well, that can limit my raking, all right. But I ain't turning monkish for you, by Go—by George. Not you nor the apostles altogether could keep me from lusting after a pretty girl." He turned away. "It might help if you stopped swinging your legs like that, though."

"Oh, dear." Lucinda stood up and smoothed out her skirts. "It's hard to remember sometimes. The freedom can be quite intoxicating, it seems. Of course no lady . . . but then, our particular situation . . . the familiarity and all. You must admit the circumstance is unique."

"To say the least," he concurred, grinning now at her efforts to look the proper female, when she wore no gloves, had no hairpins to bring order to her tumbled curls, and possessed no fichu to stuff in the low neckline of her gown.

Lucinda made her hands stop fluttering and simply stood erect, recalling days with a backboard. "So what have you decided to do about the fire damage, my lord?"

"Actually I was hoping you could wave your magic wand and restore Stanford House to its former glory, from crystal chandeliers to priceless carpets."

"I think you are confusing me with a fairy godmother or a genie in a bottle. They don't exist, you know," she told him as if imparting a great truth.

"But angels and devils and miscellaneous in-between sorts do?"

"Of course. I thought we'd covered all that before. Oh, you were just teasing, weren't you? No one has ever . . . Anyway, my assignment is to help make you a better person, not improve your living conditions. So where will you start?"

The earl ran a hand through his hair. "Hang it, I haven't the foggiest. I'm tempted to shut the place up and take lodgings. Be cheaper in the long run, rather than sinking everything I own into this barracks. Foolish for just one man. My mother hates London; she'll never come."

"Why don't you sell it if you care so little?"

He laughed without humor. "Don't you think my father would have sold it ages ago if it weren't part of the entail? Besides, who said I don't care about the old wreck? I simply cannot afford it. Were I to start restorations, just paying for the materials would strain my finances so that I couldn't afford a place to sleep in the meantime. I'd be back in the stables. I don't care what you have to say about mangers and such, I am not spending another night with my horses."

"But if Stanford House were in good repair, you could rent it out for the season at some exorbitant fee that would cover the cost of refurbishing the mansion. Grosvenor Square is the prime location to launch debutantes, you know. A few years of that and everything would be paid for."

"Fine, and what am I supposed to do during those few years, hire myself as majordomo in my own house?"

"You could go home."

"I am home, or what's left of it."

"The Abbey. Wiltshire. You could leave while repairs are being made here, go see about your estates, make something of them. I know you can if you only try."

Kerry looked at her through narrowed eyes. "That's what you wanted from the first, isn't it, to get me away from the temptations of the city? You think I'll turn into a dutiful son if I'm out of the fleshpot, that I'll take tea with the vicar and his wife, marry some bran-faced squire's daughter, and raise a parcel of God-fearing, law-abiding, frugal farmers. I begin to think this whole fire business suits you to a cow's thumb."

"*I* wasn't the one who fell asleep with a lit cigar in my hand," she retorted.

He still looked suspicious, but said, "It makes no never mind. I cannot bring this place up to any kind of standard, and I cannot hope to do anything at all for the Abbey. If you knew anything about mortgages and such, you'd know that every shilling the place earns has to go to the bank just to pay the interest on the loans. I was hoping to put it off for my mother's lifetime, but sooner or later I am going to have to petition to break the entailment so I can sell the blasted place, just to meet the obligations."

"You'd sell your son's birthright?"

"The devil take it, I don't have any son!"

"And aren't likely to at this rate," she muttered, then: "Hmm. What's this, do you think?" She was staring at a water-stained picture that had peeled back in its frame.

"Just one of my father's hunting prints, nothing even remotely valuable. He cut them out of magazines, just to fill the wall space once the paintings were gone."

"No, not the print. The painting under it."

Kerry came over. "What painting? Let me see." He scraped off the rest of the hunting print. "By George, there really is a painting under there. I can see why the governor covered the thing up. Deuced offputting, all that blood and gore."

"He seems familiar," Lucinda said, standing so close to Kerry she could have touched him, if she could have touched him.

"Who, the poor martyr chap on the cross? Did you ever get to meet . . . ?"

"No, the artist's name. Cannoli, is it?"

Kerry grabbed the picture down off the wall, frame and all, and rushed over to the window. "My God, it is! Lucy, this is the missing masterpiece from the Italian school. Cannoli taught Leonardo! Why, if this is genuine, it's worth a fortune! My father must have covered it up to hide it from his creditors, then forgot to tell anyone."

"Is it part of the entailment?" Lucinda called to him as he raced around the room, ripping scenes of horses and hounds out of frames. He brought two more oil paintings over to the window, though neither was as distinguished as the Cannoli.

"None of the furnishings were ever mentioned in the legal papers; that's how my father managed to dispose of so many antiques. I wonder why he kept these."

"For you, I suppose."

"Lucy, do you know what this means? I'll have to have them appraised, of course, but, my word, the missing masterpiece! Lucy, I could kiss you!"

And he forgot that there really wasn't any body there, and did. And felt something. It wasn't flesh and blood, but it was warm and it sent shivers through him. Lucy must have felt something, too, for she blushed like any pure maiden. Then she disappeared, like any phantasm.

Chapter Nine

The solicitor was nearly as excited as the earl.

"My lord, I cannot tell you how pleased I am. Why, the firm of Stenross and Stenross has been serving the Somerfields since our inception. I cannot express my sorrow over the recent situation. You *have* received my communications, haven't you?"

Kerry studied his fingernails.

"About the bank and the Abbey home woods? How they are demanding the trees be cut down and sold to pay something toward the debts? The wood being the last unentailed asset, they are growing quite insistent."

The deer and the quail, the yule logs and the tree houses—the debts. "That will no longer be necessary."

"Indeed, indeed." The elderly man polished his spectacles. "The paintings will have to be authenticated, of course, but I believe we might expect in excess of five thousand pounds. I think I have a buyer for the Cannoli among my own clients, a very well-respected collector, don't you know, so we might avoid public auction and all the notoriety that entails."

"I'm sure you'll think of everything, Mr. Stenross. I have always found your company to be most efficient and discreet."

The solicitor preened. "Too kind, my lord. The profit from the sale of the Cannoli *is* to satisfy some of the outstanding interest on the Abbey mortgage, then?" If Mr. Stenross sounded hesitant, he was all too aware of the Stanford flaw, a fatal tendency to gamble away any income.

"Yes, and this other piece"—another massacred saint, this one sprouting arrows like a hedgehog— "should bring in enough to complete the repairs to the Grosvenor Square house. I'll leave it with you, if you don't mind, along with what funds I can spare now, and ask you to look over the bills as they come due."

Mr. Stenross rubbed his hands. "Of course, of course, my lord. I can have my son oversee the whole project if you wish. He gets restless in these stuffy offices, don't you know."

"That will be excellent. Thank you again."

"We are always happy to serve." Especially when the serving involved saving one of the noble houses, both the structure and the succession. Mr. Stenross was one of those who still believed that the aristocracy was one of England's treasures, to be preserved for future generations like any other decrepit landmark. "And the third painting, my lord? I do not recognize the name, but the style is very popular right now. It should bring in enough to make some of those needful repairs at the Abbey." He was hopeful; things had been going so well, the earl being so reasonable, so responsible, so unlike himself.

His lordship shook his head.

"Then may I suggest the Consols?" Stenross put forward. "A bit of steady income here and there never comes amiss." That was optimism indeed.

The earl was still studying the third picture. A saint—he had a gold halo—was on the ground amid some shrubbery and flowers. He was asleep this time, Kerry thought, for there was no blood, and the figure wore a contented smile. A cherub with rosy cheeks and flaxen curls floated overhead, like a guardian angel watching out for bandits or wolves or Romans. Something about the cherub reminded the earl of Lucy; perhaps it was the innocence around the eyes. "No," he heard himself saying, "I do not want to put this one on the block unless I have to. Lock it away somewhere, will you, until Stanford House is ready for it. If it's possible, I'd like to save this one . . . for my son." There, that should at least earn Lucy a hairpin. He felt good, until the other man started beaming.

"Oh, my lord, that's the finest news I could have heard. I never believed—that is, let me extend my heartiest congratulations and wish you every—"

"Not yet, Stenross," the earl interrupted the other's effusions. "I meant someday. And if I find myself up the River Tick before then, well, the painting will have to go. Is that clear?"

"Of course, of course, but let us pray for the best, shall we? Now, my lord, where might I send information regarding the sale of the other two, and questions that might arise about the work at Stanford House? Have you found lodgings yet, or shall you be staying with friends?"

The earl cleared his throat. "You may, ah, send all communications to me at Stanford Abbey, Wiltshire. I'll stop there awhile and look into the mess. Only for the duration of the hammering and painting in Grosvenor Square, you understand."

Not only did Lucy appear with her hair tamed from its wanton look—to the earl's mixed feelings—but now she had a bonnet. A tiny, saucy hat with a cherry bow at her cheek, it was just the thing for a curricle ride out of town.

77

"And you won't be cold? I could have bricks . . ."
She just laughed.

The earl had spent a busy morning after conferring with Mr. Stenross's son about the repairs. He hired the contracting firm young Mr. Stenross had recommended, and called at one or two furniture warehouses. He visited his tailor, who welcomed him with delight, having received payment in full just the day before. Stanford was promised at least three sets of clothes, for evening, riding, and daytime, within the week. He also purchased ready-made shirts for the first time in his life, and a supply of cravats, handkerchiefs, and smallclothes. Locke luckily had a beaver hat that suited him, and the glovers had two pairs that fit almost perfectly. Demby would just have to do his best with the earl's sooty shoes and boots; there wasn't time to be fitted for new ones.

Demby would follow later in a hired carriage with the new clothes and whatever was reclaimable of the earl's smoke-permeated wardrobe; Kerry was eager to be off, now that he had made the decision.

He planned to make the trip in easy stages, not caring to leave his champion matched bays in indifferent hands, not wanting to arrive with job horses.

Lucy joined him outside of London, after the bays had run the fidgets out. Thank goodness, for the earl's hands jerked at the reins when she suddenly appeared by his side on the curricle's narrow seat. After bringing the high-bred cattle back under control, Kerry was able to appreciate his companion's glowing smile. This wasn't such a bad idea after all, stopping in at the Abbey, if it ended all that nagging and brought the chit so much pleasure. He supposed he'd wake up from this bizarre dream someday, but for now he could just enjoy her excitement.

"You see, I've never driven in a curricle before. How I used to envy those lucky girls out for rides with their dashing beaus, to be sitting so high and going so fast. And the fortunate men, to have control of such exquisite horses. None were as fine as yours, of course."

For a moment Kerry was tempted to offer her the reins, which was astounding since he had never let a female touch the ribbons of his carriage yet. What was even more astounding was that he forgot she wasn't really there. She was in Derby, waiting for Gabriel to blow his horn. He shook his head.

"You didn't have any beaus to take you driving? I cannot believe all the men of Derby are wantwits."

She giggled. "Oh, I do not believe I was very attractive to the gentlemen, being plump and pale and dowdy. But that wouldn't have mattered. Papa did not believe in fast horses, you see, or in dashing young men. He thought they were all fortune hunters. He also believed that fancy dresses and jewels encouraged a miss to put on airs, and that dancing encouraged young people in licentiousness. So I was never permitted to attend the local assemblies and such, where I could have met those whips."

"Deuce take it, no wonder you ran off with a loose screw like Anders."

"I do hope I would have made a wiser choice had I more experience, but I think I would have run away with anyone, rather than marry Lord Halbersham. He was old and mean, with hair in his nose, and had buried three wives before."

"Good grief, why would your father accept his offer? You were—you are—young enough to wait for others. And with a decent dowry, even plain girls find better partis than that."

"His title was higher than ours."

"Begging your pardon, but your father sounds a curst rum touch."

"Oh, no, he is a good man. Everyone says so. He supports the local foundling hospital and gives money to the church for new pews. His tenants are treated fairly and the servants always have enough to eat. Father is a great believer in noblesse oblige, the responsibilities of the privileged class to look after those who depend on them."

"I *have* heard the term, ma'am," Kerry said with a distinct chill in his voice.

"Oh? Then of course you have schools for your tenants' children. My father did not believe in education for the lower orders; no matter how I tried to convince him otherwise, he held that it gave them ideas above their station."

The horses suddenly pulled at their bits. Kerry forced himself to relax. "Demmed cow-handed driving," he muttered. "That's what comes of having a woman aboard." When the horses were in stride again, he continued: "My tenants are in the care of my bailiff, Wilmott. I am sure he sees to their needs."

"Then *I* am sure there is a school. And a doctor, of course."

"Wilmott manages as he sees fit. Competent fellow, been with me for years."

"If he is so competent, how come your rents have been declining for those same years and tenants keep moving on?"

"Damn—dash it, the whole nation's been in a decline, haven't you heard? It's not *my* fault farm prices are down. And I don't have the funds to do anything about the other stuff, roofs and floods and outdated equipment. You've seen the way I live. Hell, my tenants are most likely living better than I do."

"Then I take it there is no school," Lucinda commented softly, which was the last conversation for a while.

Late in the afternoon, when Kerry was thinking of seeking accommodations for the night, Lucinda told him to take a farm track off to the right.

"What, is there an inn there? I prefer one on the main road that's more used to dealing with fine horseflesh."

"Just turn here, do."

"Oh, you need to use the necessary. Why didn't you say so? I could have pulled over anytime these last miles. Strange, I wouldn't have thought a ghost or whatever would have to—"

"Just drive!" she ordered, blushing furiously.

He turned, but kept teasing. "After all, you don't eat or drink, do you?"

She wasn't listening. That is, she was listening, but not to him. Then he could hear the noise, too, screams coming from a short distance away.

"What . . . ?"

Lucy told him to keep going; the shouting sounded closer. He pulled the horses to a walk, and felt for the pistol in his pocket. When they rounded a bend in the narrow road he could see a group of boys gathered around a smallish pond. The place looked to be the perfect swimming hole—if it were summer and if the boys knew how to swim. Apparently they didn't, for they were shouting on the bank while one of their number bobbed up and down in the water.

"Hell and damnation!" Kerry swore while Lucy urged him to hurry. He jumped out of the curricle, leaving the bays to stand alone—thank goodness they were tired—and ran toward the scene. The boys on land fled into the surrounding woods, likely afraid of being caught playing too near the water, Kerry supposed. The figure in the pond was barely struggling. "Hang on," the earl shouted, looking for a long branch or something to hold out to the boy.

"You'll have to go in after him," Lucy yelled.

"Dammit, you're the supernatural one of us," Kerry yelled back, throwing his greatcoat to the ground, "why can't you part the waters or something?"

He jumped in, boots and all, and swam the short distance to the center of the pond. He couldn't see the child anywhere.

"He's gone down, just ahead of you," Lucy called from shore.

The earl dove, came up for air, and dove again. This time his hands touched something, so he hung on and kicked upward. He got to the surface, raised the dead weight in his arms, and started to turn the air blue with his curses.

"You promised!" Lucy screamed, holding her hands over her ears.

"It's a bloody dog!" Kerry roared back. "I ruined my only set of clothes and my Hessians for a dog!" And he prepared to throw the animal back into the depths.

Lucy shrieked, "Don't! It's one of God's creatures, you heartless libertine!"

Kerry was already wet, and he already had the animal in his arms, so he swam closer to the bank and then waded ashore, dropping the small hound-mix at Lucy's feet. "Here." He even untied the rock from around the pup's neck before returning to the curricle to check on his bays and dry himself off with the lap robe. He was pulling on one of the new ready-made shirts from his valise, when Lucy called to him.

"Kerry, he's not breathing!" Her eyes were huge, imploring.

"That's your department, angel. I did what I could."

"Kerry, please." A tear was starting to trickle down one cheek, leaving a path through the rouge.

"What do you expect me to— Oh, no, not the kiss-of-life bit again. Demby was bad enough, Lucy, but a dog? Never!"

The dog was whiskery and wet and smelled of swamp. Worse, when Kerry was done, the mutt crawled over and licked Lucy's hand.

"Of all the ungrateful— How come he can see you and no one else can?"

"He can see me only now, while he's so close to

death. He'll forget in a minute and won't notice me at all."

Sure enough, the dog, no more than a puppy really, soon whimpered to Kerry, wagging his tail.

"Oh, no, you don't," the earl commanded. "You go find a softer touch. Go on home now, sir."

"He hasn't got a home. He's been living in the woods, close to starvation. If he goes near that farm again, those boys will only try to drown him again, or the farmer will shoot him for bothering the chickens."

"Damn and blast, woman, what do you expect me to do about it?"

So the dog sat between them on the curricle's seat while the earl carefully backed the horses and returned them to the main road.

"He's cold."

Kerry looked down, and the dog was indeed shivering. "With all the heat at your command, can't you . . . ? No, I suppose not. That would be too easy." Soon the puppy was nestled next to the earl's second-to-last clean shirt, buttoned under his greatcoat. No respectable hostelry would take him in like this, the earl considered, so he'd be bedding down in a stable somewhere with his horses after all. But the rouge was gone entirely from Lucy's creamy cheeks, and her lips were now a natural pink color, spread in a happy grin. Kerry felt warm, despite the weather, his wet boots, and the damp dog.

"And it's only a few days until Demby gets here with the rest of my things anyway," the earl conceded.

"Demby's not coming, my lord. He'll send your clothes and belongings when he gets a chance, I suppose."

"Not coming? What gammon is this? Of course Demby is coming."

Lucy bit her lip. "Uh, remember that lottery ticket you gave him?"

Chapter Ten

"Just look at you! Is this any way to enter a lady's drawing room? And without telling us you were coming!"

"Hello, Mother. I am delighted to see you, too," Kerry said, lightly kissing the powdered cheek Lady Margaret Stanford reluctantly offered.

Her nose wrinkled. "What's that odor? And what is that creature with you?"

"It's my new valet. Shall we set a style, do you think? His name is Lucky."

"Oh, you're still a tease." Aunt Clara chuckled, opening her arms for a hug, then thinking better of it. She shrugged and permitted the embrace, so she could whisper in his ear: "Nigel says you'll need your sense of humor around this place."

"I see that everything is the same here." The same overheated drawing room, the same caustic tongue, and the same superfluity of servants, with one coming to take the dog to the kitchen, one to fetch tea, one to notify the housekeeper to see to the master's bedroom. Even the same Aunt Clara, still all draped in mourning crepe for Uncle Nigel after twenty years.

"Nothing is the same, which you would know if you read my letters," the dowager Lady Stanford announced. "We have had to close the east wing due to dampness, cancel the annual open house because the grounds are in such deplorable condition, and I am ashamed to show my face in church after the vicar was nearly killed by a falling roof tile. I have been suffering from an agitation of the nerves for weeks now."

Kerry was suffering from days in an open carriage, nights in various barns, and an incipient head cold. He spoke a little more sharply than he intended: "It's a wonder you don't choose to reside in the dower house, then, if this one distresses you so."

"What, that pawky place? I could hardly entertain. Besides, think of the expense of operating two houses."

Kerry thought of his mother supporting herself on her own widow's pension and leaving this pile with a mere caretaking staff. Talk of pipe dreams! The only abode suitable for the Countess of Stanford, according to the Countess of Stanford, was Stanford Abbey, every moldy corner of it. Then again, if the dowager chose to use her annuity to keep the Abbey in appearances, how could he argue? Of course, he hadn't seen much evidence of her contributions. The drive was so pitted he had to get down and lead his pair through the ruts, for fear of damaging the curricle's wheels. His first view of the Abbey itself, with its hodgepodge of styles and additions, also showed boarded windows, ropes across areas presumably in danger from flying tiles, and shrubbery gone wild. Doors were hanging loose on the stable, and the large indoor staff was in shabby livery.

"Everything will be fine now that you are home, Kieren. We shall open the ballroom and the conservatory, of course. Rehire the gardeners, order new draperies for the public rooms, and—"

"Hold, Mother. If you wish to apply your widow's pension to the improvements, I'll be forever in your debt, for I haven't resources for any of those things."

Lady Stanford did not offer a penny more of her substantial income. "Of course you do. We heard all about your winning at the races."

Kerry wondered how they could have heard so quickly. He glanced at Aunt Clara's nodding gray head. Did she really hear from Uncle Nigel? He'd have to ask Lucy about that.

"I'm sorry to disappoint you, Mother, but I had some necessary expenses of my own. And you cannot have heard of the fire at Stanford House." Or the paintings, he hoped. "My finances are already strained."

"Then why did you come home?" his loving mother asked ungraciously. "I'm already at the edge of ruin, trying to hold house for you while you live the high life in London."

Where Kerry wished he'd stayed. "I know, Mother, and I truly appreciate your generosity. I fully intend to repay you, though I cannot see how at this moment. I came as you requested, to see if there is anything to be done to make the properties more profitable."

"I am sure Wilmott is wringing every shilling out of the place already," Lady Stanford told him angrily.

"Nigel says he's cheating you, Kerry," Aunt Clara put in, earning her a scowl from the dowager.

"That's neither here nor there, Kieren. You'll not make a go of farming. Your father never managed to. You'll just have to marry a rich female. Even your father managed *that*." She spoke with more than her usual degree of bitterness, then cracked her lined face into a smile. "At least you're better favored than the old windbag was. The local girls will be tripping over themselves for an introduction. Naturally I'll make sure you meet only the ones with generous portions. With your looks and the title and my careful attention to those details of dowries, we'll have Stanford Abbey in prime twig in no time."

"Mother, I have no inten—" Kerry began to object.

"Don't think I mean to hang on your coattails either. When I know you are secure, and my accounts have been settled, I'll take a little place in Bath. After a year or two, of course. Your new countess will need me here to show her how to go on before that."

"Mother—"

"Now, let me see, there's Westcott's girl. They were hoping to bring that duke up to scratch, but nothing came of it. And Lady Prudlow's granddaughters will be visiting her for the holidays. We'll have to hold a ball, I think. Yes, that should do it, rather than waiting for invitations." Suddenly the dowager's lined face crumpled in mid-strategy. "My jewels! How can I entertain all those well-dowered females without my jewels? I'll look no-account to Lady Prudlow and that shrewish Isabella Westcott. Oh, how can I ever show my face in the neighborhood without a tiara?" she sobbed.

Clara shook her head but went for the vinaigrette. Kerry took his mother's hand—ringless, he noted with remorse—and swore to make things right. He very carefully did not swear to marry an heiress, but he did vow to do his utmost to recover the jewels his mother had so selflessly sacrificed on his behalf. "Right after dinner I'll start going over Wilmott's books and see—"

"Dinner!" the dowager shrieked. "We're having company for dinner. Look at the time, and I'm not dressed. You must be tired from your journey, Kieren, so I'll have the housekeeper send a tray to your room."

Aunt Clara loudly whispered, "Goldy Flint is coming, the smuggler. I told you so."

"Mr. Gideon Flint is a retired wine merchant, I'll have you know. But if you do not wish to sit to table with us tonight, I shall make your excuses. No place has been laid for you anyway," she sniped, "since you did not see fit to notify us of your visit."

"I am sure a place can be laid for the head of the household, Mother. I'll leave you to dress, then, and see what I can do about repairing my wardrobe. I wouldn't want to embarrass your company by appearing in all my dirt."

Kerry needn't have worried; his odd ensemble fit right in. Aunt Clara was in her unrelieved black, looking like a plump little crow. Lady Stanford wore feathers and flounces, ribbons and ruffles, any number of gewgaws designed to camouflage her lack of jewels. Mr. Flint, whose sobriquet actually came from a gold tooth, not the amazing amount of fobs and pendants he had dangling from his expansive chest, was likewise overdressed in white satin knee breeches. The breeches looked like sausage casings, with the prosperous Mr. Flint stuffed and ready for the pan. His waistcoat was cerise with, naturally, gold embroidery, and his coat was pale blue satin. He resembled nothing so much as a masquerade-goer dressed as a hot-air balloon.

Kerry would have traded. His own outfit, hastily assembled by one of the ubiquitous footmen pressed into valet duty, was culled from the attic trunks. The brocaded lemon and scarlet frock coat was his father's, so it pulled across his shoulders and gaped across his waist. He would have left it unbuttoned except the only waistcoat the doltish footman could find in a hurry was the butler's Sunday best, complete with gravy stains. The peach satin smallclothes were Uncle Nigel's, twenty years in mothballs, and smelling like thirty. Kerry's shoes were a pair he'd outgrown in his university days, so pinched unmercifully. At least the shirt and stockings were new.

The earl was tempted to wonder if Mr. Flint's wardrobe had been lost in a fire, too, except his style of speech seemed to match his style of dress. Without so much as a by-your-leave, the nabob—he could be a pirate, for all Kerry knew—joined the dowager in a discussion of the local debutantes.

"I was wondering your opinion of this wine," Kerry interrupted, to put paid to this conversation, especially in front of the waiting footmen. He also wanted to see if the old rasher of wind knew anything about vintages at all.

"Don't worry about the wine, my boy. I made sure your mother has only the best. You put your mind to finding a wealthy gel, eh?" Goldy crammed another forkful of stuffed prawns into his mouth before turning back to the dowager. "I think your best bet is Westcott's chit, Margie. Five thousand a year, and more if that aunt names her beneficiary."

Margie? No one had ever called Margaret, Countess Stanford, anything but My Lady in Kerry's lifetime. Not even his father. Now some fat old free trader was calling her by diminutives? Aunt Clara was right, by George. His mother was so lonely, so desperate for company, she was taking up with a wine merchant. And a deuced good one, to judge by the Madeira. Meantime, the mushroom was discussing his, the Earl of Stanford's, marriage prospects!

"Wedding a female for her money is a caddish thing to do," he stated in a pause of their conversation. "Degrading for both parties. I do not believe in marriages of convenience." How could he, after knowing Lucy's story?

Aunt Clara was silently applauding, but his mother was astounded. "Don't be a jackanapes. It's the way of the world. And how else can you hope to bring this place about? It's not as though you've gone and thrown your heart over the windmill like some ninnyhammer either." She pointedly ignored her sister-in-law. "So you might as well marry a rich girl."

"Your mother's in the right of it, lad," Mr. Flint put in. "Fellow's got to think with his head, not just his ba—heart. No one said all heiresses have to be antidotes. Leave it to your mother to find you a pretty one. 'Sides, there's not a girl on this earth so platter-faced she wouldn't look bonny in a count-ess's tiara."

The dowager's fork clattered onto her plate and her lip started to tremble.

"Aunt Clara," Kerry said loudly, "I know you be-lieve in ghosts, but do you believe there is a heaven and hell?" That was the first topic that came to mind, being on his own mind often these days.

"I do not know about hell," Aunt Clara answered after a moment's reflection. "I have never known anyone that bad. But of course there is heaven, dear. Uncle Nigel is only waiting to go until I join him there."

The dowager was over her lapse and glaring. Not only had Kerry exposed Mr. Flint to Clara's dotti-ness, but religion was *not* a proper subject for the dinner table. Kerry raised his wineglass to her. "And you, Mother, what think you of the afterlife?"

"I cannot imagine anything drearier than spend-ing the rest of eternity in heaven with one's poor relations"—a frown toward Aunt Clara—"unless it's spending it in hell with your father. I refuse to contemplate either."

"And no reason you should, at your tender years." Mr. Flint reached out a fat hand and patted the dowager's arm. Kerry almost choked and Aunt Clara smirked.

"And you, Mr. Flint? Have you thought about the hereafter?"

Gideon took a long swallow of wine. "Well, m'lord, I've thought about it, all right. I like to be prepared, don't you know. It's always paid in my business. I *think* those stories about reward and punishment are tales to scare the kiddies. Just in case there are fleecy clouds, though, with dancing girls and flowing wines, I've been paying my dues at the church."

"You hope to buy your way into heaven?"

"No, they say you can't take it with you. This way it'll be waiting there for me."

After dinner Mr. Flint excused himself. "Hope you don't mind my leaving you to take your port alone, m'lord. Lady Stanford expects me in the parlor, don't you know. We get up a hand or two of piquet. Helps to pass the time."

Kerry had been thinking of a way to warn the man off. The chap was as vulgar as a Punch-and-Judy skit, and as likable, but Lady Stanford and a midnight-merchant? Preposterous. "Fine, fine," he said. "You go on and join the ladies. I wanted to start looking over the books this evening anyway. We'll be too busy for such quiet evenings for some time now, I expect, with the countess planning that ball to entertain every eligible female in the county. Enjoy the card game while you may. You will likely be the last company we invite for a while." There, he congratulated himself, that wasn't too broad a hint.

It was so narrow, Mr. Flint missed it entirely. "Oh, I ain't company, m'lord. Margie treats me like one of the family. You can call me Goldy, lad."

Lucy was ecstatic. "What a wonderful place! It's perfect!"

"Perfect? It's shabby and run-down, overstaffed and undersupervised. These ledgers resemble the Rosetta stone, and the bailiff has been robbing me blind. My aunt has bats in her bell tower, my mother is on the verge of the misalliance of the century with a free-booter who has the run of the place, and you think it's perfect?"

"Oh, yes! Think of all the opportunities to do good deeds!"

Chapter Eleven

The ledger books were not improved by the earl's staying up all night to pore over them. Neither was his cold. The fireplace in his bedchamber wasn't working, according to a footman who reported that chimneys in the unused chambers were not cleaned in the interests of economy, milord. Milord snapped back that economies could dashed well begin in the servants' hall, not his bedchamber. Which conversation, dutifully reported below stairs, had the staff spending a restless night, too, fearful of losing positions or what few comforts the Abbey offered.

Unable to sleep, the glum footmen heard their master talking to himself downstairs in the estate office half the night. Two handed in their resignations before breakfast. Why wait to be dismissed when the employer was not only a nipfarthing, but touched in the upper works besides? Cook huddled in her cot all night with the cooking sherry, praying to be delivered from the Abbey ghosts, so breakfast didn't promise to be any great shakes anyway.

Without coffee Kerry had even less success deciphering the books. For the life of him, he couldn't see where Wilmott was putting the dowager's money to use. His pride nagged at him, that his mother was using her own pension to pay for his household expenses. Every manly sensibility was offended, as if he'd been hiding behind a woman's skirts, living as a gigolo, marrying for money. Furthermore, if her income were intact, she might take herself off to Bath, to meet gout-ridden generals and dyspeptic dukes. Anything but wealthy merchants of questionable backgrounds.

Lady Stanford never went to London, she said, because she could not tolerate the endless embarrassing gossip about her only son and his raffish ways, which she managed to keep very well informed about here in the country. Kerry suspected the dowager's rustication was also caused by an embarrassment of funds. She could not make a splash in the metropolis, and she liked being a big fish in the small pond of Derby society. Kerry made a note to write to Mr. Stenross, inquiring into the exact specifications of his mother's pension. Meanwhile, the idea of sending Lady Stanford to Bath appealed to Lord Stanford, and not just to get her away from Goldy Flint.

So where was the dowager's money going? Was she paying servants' wages off the books, or merchants' bills in cash that was never recorded in the household accounts? Absurd, considering the amounts charged to the estate. There appeared to be enough servants to keep the Tower of London clean and enough foodstuffs to satisfy the Carlton House set. For two elderly ladies? No, Wilmott had to be inflating the expenses and pocketing the dowager's cash, then draining the estate income to pay the bills. No wonder the mortgages were never met. No wonder Kerry never saw a shilling of profit.

Wilmott had to go. At worst he was a crook; at best he was an inefficient manager and a terrible bookkeeper.

Wilmott came to give his notice before Kerry even sent for him.

"Now that you're here, my lord, I can leave with a free conscience. I did my best for you, with no thanks. The land's gone to ruin while you and yourn live high on the hog, and it ain't right, I tell you. Disheartening to a fellow it is, to see his work gone for naught but gaming debts and fancy togs. Did you answer when I wrote as how the income had to go back into the property for improvements? Nary a word. And when I said expenses were too high? Nary a word. Well, now you're back to see for yourself, and good riddance to you, I say. I've had an offer from a gentleman t'other side of the county. Wants to raise sheep. Be a relief to work for someone who wants to raise anything but Cain. And don't worry about paying my salary, you haven't for the last two quarters anyway."

When the echo of the slamming door died, Lord Stanford hunched forward and put his head in his hands. Either the fellow was a fine actor, or Kerry's last chance of making sense out of the estate business had just deserted him. He blew his nose and made a note to pay the man his back wages if he did, indeed, deserve them. Lud, he needed a drink.

"You need some hot soup and a warm bed," Lucy told him, appearing at the end of his desk, looking concerned.

He blew his nose again. "No. Too much to do. I don't suppose you know any magic tricks to fix this mess?" He waved a hand at the ledgers. "I know, you're a demon, not a wizard. Maybe I'd do better to go upstairs and ask Uncle Nigel's advice."

"About Uncle Nigel . . ."

"Not now, Lucy, I've got to do some thinking."

Kerry's immediate concerns were finding an honest, intelligent bailiff, redeeming his mother's jewels, which debt weighed heavily on his mind, and visiting the local haberdashery. The haberdasher came first.

The drive through his property to the village of Standing Falls made him realize like nothing before the extent of his difficulties. A new waistcoat he could afford, and trousers and a superfine coat that needed only minor tailoring. But the fallen roofs, the deserted cottages, the shoeless children, the unfriendly faces on people he'd known all his life—how could he ever hope to fix all that?

Lucy wanted to talk about the Golden Rule. "You know, do unto others . . ."

"I know that, blast it. Don't you think I'd like to make everything right? Or have you painted me so black that I don't care about the plight of these people? It's a wonder you haven't given up on me, then," he added morosely, falling deeper into the doldrums with every new reminder of the poverty around them.

"You could afford to smile, at least. I'm sure *you'd* feel better if people were pleasant to you."

So he waved and tried to smile, with his red, drippy nose and heavy head. The villagers just shook their heads. Drink must have addled the rake's brain box, on top of everything else. Grinning like a fool and talking to hisself. No hope there.

Kerry felt better after the visit to the haberdasher's, especially when his cash payment brought the first sign of friendliness he'd seen. Vanity might be a sin, but a fellow's amour propre suffered grievously in castoffs. Now he was ready to face the shopkeeper in Farley whose chits he held, in place of his mother's jewels. Redeeming the diamonds might take the last of his latest windfall, but a grown man should not stand indebted to his own mother.

Gilmore's on Center Street was almost as discreet as the jeweler Kerry patronized in London when temporarily in dun territory. There was a silver tea service in the window—Kerry was relieved not to recognize the inscribed crest—and some gilt-framed portraits hanging on the walls over shelves of vases, epergnes, and candelabra. Glass cases with velvet-lined shelves held rows of timepieces, snuffboxes, and any kind of jewelry a lovesick swain might purchase to win a lady's heart, any kind of trinket a down-at-the-heels lady might pop to earn a few pounds.

The shop wasn't terribly busy. A young country-dressed couple was looking at rings; a foppish gentleman of middling years in yellow cossack trousers was surveying a tray of quizzing glasses.

Mr. Gilmore left the coxcomb experimenting with each of the lenses to greet his newest—and most prestigious-looking—customer. Kerry's stature and bearing proclaimed his nobility, even if his Hessians would never be the same and his many-caped greatcoat still showed dog footprints. The bespectacled shopkeeper was even more delighted when Kerry presented his card.

"The Earl of Stanford," he read loudly, when Kerry's intention in handing over the card was to maintain his anonymity. Gilmore even bowed at the waist, in case any of his other clientele missed the aristocratic presence in the little shop. The dandy inspected Kerry through one of the looking glasses, like some new specimen of insect, until the earl glared back at him.

"Just so, milord, honored indeed," Gilmore was prattling. "You must be here for her ladyship's diamonds."

"Yes," Kerry replied, trying for a bit of subtlety. "I understand she brought them in to be cleaned."

"Cleaned, is it?" Gilmore chuckled as he wiped his spectacles. "That's the first time I've heard it called that. I'll just fetch them from out back. I never do put her ladyship's goods up for sale, you know, for she always manages to buy them back before any big party. I suppose you'll be having a ball up at the Abbey, now you're to home."

Kerry did not respond, wasting a haughty set-down stare at the gabble-grinder's back. Mr. Gilmore was too excited at having a real earl in his store to notice the icy silence. "Too bad about the gambling," he shouted from behind the partitioning curtain. "They say it's like a disease."

"You, sir, are impertinent," the Earl of Stanford snapped back when Gilmore placed the necklace, bracelet, ring, and tiara on the counter. Gads, first Wilmott, now this bumpkin of a shopkeeper. Did every rustic feel free to comment on Kerry's gaming habits? He turned to scowl at the young couple, who were looking at him as if he were an ax mur-derer. He almost shouted that his debts were all paid and he'd given up the practice, by Jupiter. And if the man-milliner didn't stop viewing Kerry through that eyepiece, he'd soon find his one en-larged orb closed by Kerry's fist. As for the counter-jumper, no, that was beneath the earl's dignity. He took out his wallet, eager to get this transaction over and done with.

When Kerry turned back to lay his blunt on the glass case, his motions were arrested by the sight of Lucy sitting on the counter, hammering at his mother's diamond necklace with her shoe.

"What the deuce are you doing now? Put that down, I say!"

At which the tulip dropped the three quizzing glasses he'd been stuffing in his pocket while Gilmore's attention was on the earl. He fled, Gilmore in pursuit calling for the watch. The young couple shook their heads and left.

Unaware, Lucy was battering away at the dia-monds, to absolutely no avail, of course, since her shoe kept passing right through them. Kerry snatched the necklace out of her reach anyway, and held it up to the window to make sure there was no damage. Then he reached for one of the quizzing glasses the would-be thief had dropped and studied the diamonds even more closely.

"By all that's holy, they're paste!"

"Of course they are, my lord," Gilmore said, returning and mopping his bald head while he caught his breath. "Do you think I would lend the countess this mere pittance if they were real?" The pittance he indicated was almost Kerry's entire bankroll. "Her ladyship would never pawn her real jewels, just the ones she wears every day without fear of losing them." He put the necklace, ring, and bracelet into a velvet pouch, the tiara in a wooden box. "I'm sure the originals are safe at home in your vault."

Kerry was certain they were not; why would the dowager have the vapors over her copies when she had the originals to wear for that blasted ball she was planning?

Mr. Gilmore was going on: "But forgive me, my lord, I have not expressed my gratitude for your alert intervention. The thief got away, but you saved me a tidy sum in trinkets. I am in your debt."

Kerry noticed that the man did not feel indebted enough to hand back the outrageous sum he'd just pocketed for paste diamonds. Paste, for pity's sake!

"And to show my appreciation," the storekeeper was saying, "I'll give you back the rubies at no interest."

"The rubies, you say! They're entailed! Mother could never put them on tick."

"Austrian crystals, this set."

Kerry forked over the last of his ready for glass rubies, and cursed the entire ride home while Lucy's cheeks got redder. Embarrassment or returning rouge, he didn't know which, and he didn't care right then.

The real jewels were not in the vault, of course. What were there instead were receipts for gaming slips—Kerry recognized them well—in payment of which his mother had pledged her rings, bracelets, necklaces, and the diamond tiara. And *his* ruby parure and the Stanford engagement ring.

"I'll strangle her. I'll put my hands around her scrawny neck and I'll—"

"The Chinese philosopher Confucius phrased the Golden Rule in the negative: do not do to others what you wouldn't like done to you."

The dowager hadn't been pawning her valuables to make ends meet, she'd been meeting gambling debts. Worst of all, the name on the receipts, the person now in possession of his mother's jewelry, and the Stanford rubies, was none other than Gideon Flint.

"Why, that . . . that dastard. That's how he got so rich, not by smuggling at all, but by diddling wealthy widows out of their gems. And that's why she lets a loose screw like that run tame at the Abbey. She's so much in his debt, she daren't say no."

"I thought she was just lonely," Lucy put in, still bending over the safe.

Kerry was *almost* too distraught to notice her rounded rear end, but he wasn't dead yet, so he paused in his ranting to admire the view. Backsliding had its advantages; Lucy wore no shift or petticoat. He sighed.

"It doesn't matter what methods that bounder used to win her trust. He holds those vouchers and I'm back in debt. I cannot let my mother be beholden to such a blackguard. Who knows what liberties a pirate like that might take? How in blue blazes I'm supposed to redeem those jewels, I'll never know. And here I was, finally caught up on the mortgages. I even thought I'd have some brass to invest in the Abbey like everyone's always nattering at me to do, so the estate could start paying again."

"Did you know Uncle Nigel had shares in a copper mine in Haiti?" Lucy straightened up, but her hair was all undone. Kerry's hands itched to run through the silky tresses, watching the red turn to gold. He sighed again—he was doing that a lot lately—and bent to look into the safe. He pulled out a partnership deed.

"Good try, Lucy, but the paper is useless. I remember my father raging on about Nigel's West Indies bubble. My uncle put most of his capital in the venture and never saw a ha'penny back. The thing went bust in slave uprisings. And even if it hadn't, his shares reverted to his partners when he drowned."

"About Uncle Nigel . . ."

"No, some worthless copper mine shares can't help me now. It's looking more and more like the home woods have to go after all. Or my horses."

Chapter Twelve

*B*oth. Kerry was going to have to sell off the timber stand after all, and the string of hunters he kept stabled at the Abbey. A quick ride around the home farm to burn off some of his fury before confronting his mother showed him how much needed to done. Even his inexperienced eye put the cost at well over what he could realize from the price of his horses. He hadn't been able to afford the hunt last year anyway; this year looked to be no different. Why should he have the nags eating their heads off in the stables, requiring grooms and exercise boys, when he had better use for the money?

Kerry surprised himself by realizing that he wouldn't mind half so much selling off his stable in order to make an investment in the future. A new plow, say, or having a work crew come in to dig that drainage ditch. But to pay his mother's gambling debts to a rogue of a neighbor who most likely fuzzed the cards besides? Now, *that* was a waste of fine horseflesh, like the prime goer under him right now. To say nothing of that woodland where his tree house still leaned precariously among the branches. Hell and tarnation!

Stanford kept riding at a furious pace, past his property line, past the small farms, past the little village, until he could see a large house on a hill. Lord Humboldt's derelict old place used to be the neighborhood's haunted house, attracting small boys who would dare each other to knock on the door or snatch a fallen chestnut from the big tree beside the windows. Now the mansion was all in lights as dusk fell, with every pane of glass shining, every shrub manicured into precision. Goldy Flint had put his money to good use.

Not quite sure of his own intentions, the earl rode up the graveled carriage path. He couldn't call the cit out; affairs of honor were for gentlemen. If there was one thing Flint wasn't, that was it. Kerry could land the man a facer, though, he thought with eager anticipation, after demanding to know the price to redeem the Stanford rubies. At this moment Lord Stanford was so angry at both his mother and her cardsharp friend that he was willing to let the dastard keep the diamonds, let the countess wear paste.

"The lands come first." Kerry almost fell off his horse when he heard himself say that aloud. He was too used to Lucy's presence. But where had such sentiment come from? Not two days ago he'd happily have consigned the estate to perdition. Must be that plaguey chit's influence there, too, making him act like a mooncalf.

Two grooms rushed forward to take his horse, and two footmen pulled open the double doors at the entrance to Flint's abode. A very proper butler in powdered wig bowed the earl into the marble hall. How many widows had the rogue swindled, Kerry wondered, to afford such a display? He snapped his riding crop against his leg.

Fortunately for Mr. Gideon Flint, the man was not at home at present. The butler informed Lord

Stanford that his employer was away on business for a few days but was certain to call on Lady Stanford at his return, unless his lordship wished to leave a message?

His lordship wished to leave a few broken noses, but he merely nodded politely and returned to his horse, which had been rubbed down and walked.

Blast! But he should have known, Kerry told himself. 'Twas a full moon; likely the old scoundrel was out on a smuggling run. Either that or he'd already heard from the servants' grapevine or that toady Gilmore that the earl was onto his lay.

The countess had certainly been apprised of the earl's foray to Gilmore's and his subsequent fury. She had taken to her room with a severe megrim, her maid reported, caused by overexhaustion with plans for the ball. Short of breath and faint-headed, she was much too ill to grant her son an interview.

"Too faint-hearted, more like," he muttered. He did direct the maid to extend his sympathy. "And tell your mistress I would not for the world have Lady Stanford jeopardize her health, so I insist there shall be no ball. I have already canceled her order for invitations." There, that should take care of that bit of nonsense, too. Undoubtedly the countess would be too weak—and too furious—to descend for dinner either, so Kerry made his excuses to Aunt Clara and rode into town to the local tavern.

The village of Standing Falls used to boast an inn and two pubs. But that was when the mill was operating, when produce wagons and delivery carts and fancy carriages made frequent trips through the village, when every house on the main street was occupied. In other words, when Stanford Abbey was prosperous and supporting the local economy. Now Standing Falls was more fallen than standing. Half the cottages were deserted, the Stanford Arms posting inn was long boarded up, and only one unprepossessing alehouse remained. The church deacons might have been gladdened at the demise of the watering places, except that the house of worship had not escaped the overall decline: the broken church steps were replaced with a series of planks and barrels.

Kerry stepped around the makeshift stairs after leaving his horse at the livery, and made his way to the building under the sign of a torrent of liquid pouring into a mug. The Falls had been at the corner before his birth, serving generations of farmers. Now it served the needs of fieldworkers, servants, tradesmen, and gentry alike.

Some of all were represented this raw November evening. A party of well-to-pass but undistinguished travelers sat at the large table at the center of the room, quietly conferring among themselves over dinner. Kerry had noted their well-appointed carriage at the livery. A red-coated soldier was slumped over his drink at the inglenook, while a clerk of some sort made notes in a pad on the opposite side of the hearth amid numerous satchels and parcels. The local blacksmith and another man Kerry did not recognize were at one end of the long plank bar, and a group of thick-soled farmers were at the other end, warming their hands over mugs of steaming ale.

No one stirred at Kerry's entry beyond a few disinterested glances, so he took a table in the corner, his back to the wall. After a longer-than-polite interval the barkeep, who was also the tavern owner, called from behind the stained wood counter, "What can I do for you, your lordship?"

The blacksmith grunted. A few of the other heads turned, then went back to their drinks.

"Good evening, Ned. And you, Charlie," with a nod to the brawny smith. "I'll have a pint and a menu."

"It's pigeon pie, steak and kidneys, or stew, same as it's been every night for dogs' years. 'Course I don't expect you to recall that, your lordship, seeing as it's been—what? Two, three years since you been here in the neighborhood?"

One of the farmers snickered, his back to the earl. Kerry ordered the steak and kidneys and then started to eat in silence after Ned slammed a dish on the table in front of him. Tacit hostility was better than any more comments about gaming debts, he supposed. And the food was good, hot, and filling, even if it was the plainest fare he'd had in ages.

One or two of the farmers left for their own suppers, and a herder came in with his dog, proceeding to share a bowl of stew with the animal. Kerry was beginning to wish he'd brought the drowned mutt Lucky along; at least he'd have someone to talk to over the meal. Of course he could go back to the Abbey and chat with Aunt Clara. Or Uncle Nigel.

The toffs at the center table were preparing to leave, wrapping mufflers, drawing on gloves, settling their bill, when Kerry next chanced to look up as an odd odor reached his nostrils. The sheepdog? The blacksmith's pipe? The ages-old pigeon pie? No, there was Lucy, looking as wanton and as luscious as ever, patting the shoulder of the redcoat near the fire.

"Stop that!" Kerry shouted in what he was horrified to discover was a loud, jealous-sounding voice that drew the attention of everyone in the room. The earl ignored the startled looks, staring beyond them at Lucy trying to brush back the soldier's hair. He did manage to lower his voice as he asked, "What the hell are you doing here? You don't belong where men are drinking!"

" 'Ere now, who are you to be insultin' one of our brave boys?" Charlie the blacksmith demanded, and one of the farmers, one of Kerry's own tenants, he thought, muttered, " 'At's right, Charlie. Ask him where *he* was during the war."

The gentlemen who were getting ready to depart

looked at one another and shrugged, then hurried about their leavetaking before the scene got ugly.

Kerry gathered his wits back from where they'd gone begging at Lucy's half-bare chest, and apologized to the room at large. "No, no, never meant to insult anyone, especially a soldier. I was just, ah, woolgathering about something else entirely. Here, Ned, pour the fellow a drink on me. In fact, buy one for everyone."

Charlie sat back on his stool, and even the sheepdog's hair lay flat again. Lucy still scowled at the earl when Ned roused the soldier enough to put a fresh glass into his left hand. Now Kerry noticed that the other sleeve was pinned up where his right arm was missing altogether. Oh, God.

"Can't you see he doesn't need another drink?" Lucy chided, trying ineffectually to stop the soldier from spilling the ale in his lap.

"Maybe he'd do better with coffee, Ned, or some hot food." Kerry reached for another coin, but all that was left was his lucky gold piece. He put it on the table.

"Keep your blunt," the barkeep said. "The lieutenant's meals are free. He lost his arm saving my nevvy's life in that heathen place."

The lieutenant may have lost his arm, but Lucy had found it for him. To the earl's horror, she was walking around the soldier with a limp, bare arm, trying somehow to affix it to his shoulder.

"Do you mean that all those missing limbs are waiting for their owners in heaven?" Kerry choked out.

One of the farmers crossed himself and Charlie shook his head. "They was right at the Abbey. Few cards short of a full deck."

But the veteran looked up and smiled sweetly at Kerry. "What a charming thought. That's something to look forward to, at any rate." He lifted his coffee cup in salute. "Thank you, Stanford."

"Johnny? John Norris? Is that really you? Of

course it is. Man, it's been ages." It had been almost ten years, in fact, since Kieren Somerfield had played cricket with the squire's sons on the village green. Kerry'd gone on to the university and then his life in London; Ralph had taken over his father's place right there in Wiltshire, but John had gone off to join the army.

"I'm deuced sorry about your arm, Johnny, and my, uh, tactlessness. I've been in a brown study here, coming home and all." To say nothing of Lucy, who seemed to be checking the clerk's baggage on the other side of the fireplace.

Johnny waved away his apologies. "Welcome back, then, my lord, and take a seat." He indicated the bench next to him.

"It's always been Kerry, John," the earl replied as he carried his drink over and sat down. "So what are you doing now?"

"Drinking. What else is there to do for a one-armed man with no prospects?"

Kerry lifted his own glass. "At least you've got a good excuse."

"Yes, I've heard of your difficulties."

The earl took another swallow. "Everyone has. I'm thinking of selling off my stables. Do you think Ralph would be interested? He used to be horse-mad."

"Still is, and still can't tell a Thoroughbred from a tinker's mule. If your cattle are as bang up to the mark as ever, I bet he'll snap them up in a flash. Be happy to talk to him about it if you wish, get back to you tomorrow."

"Thank you, I'd appreciate that." Ralph Norris would treat the nags well, at least, and he could afford to pay top dollar. Not that it made parting with the horses any easier. Not that it would solve enough of Kerry's problems.

"Not enough, eh?" Johnny asked.

Kerry figured he wasn't a mind reader, just up on the local gossip. "Not by half."

"What you need is an heiress," Lieutenant Norris firmly stated.

"Not you, too, Johnny. That's all I'm hearing, find some fubsy-faced chit whose father's got deep pockets. Old Lady Prudlow's trotting out two well-heeled antidotes again this year."

"Felicia Westcott's not fubsy-faced, and the marquis is warm enough for your needs," Johnny insisted.

"If she's such a paragon, why don't you try for her?"

"What, a second son with no title and no prospects but m'brother's charity? Old man Westcott's too downy a cove for that."

"You're right, my outlook is brighter," Kerry said bitterly. "I at least have the option of selling my title when all else fails. What will you do? Go into government work?"

"A desk job? Never. And the army is done with me, so that ends that career. I intended to be a gentleman farmer, help m'brother run the place, that kind of thing. But I depress his wife. Breeding, don't you know. Sensitive type. And big brother doesn't think I'm capable now that I have only one arm. Doesn't want me out and about lest I hurt myself worse, he says." He threw the mug of coffee into the fire, where it hissed, and called for another ale. "Do you know the best part? All those months of recuperation, lying there, do you know what I did? I read farm journals. Everything I could get my hands on, all about Coke and his new ideas, seed presses and crop rotation. Funny, huh?"

Kerry didn't laugh. "I wish someone would teach me half that stuff."

"Pigs."

Kerry looked around to see who Johnny was calling names. If his foxed young friend was starting a fight, Kerry hoped he didn't pick on the blacksmith.

Lucy was back, sitting beside Johnny, who was

oblivious of her presence. How could he not notice, when Kerry could feel the tingle from here?

"Pigs," Johnny repeated. "That's all you need to know. They're the most productive crop for your kind of land. Feed's the cheapest, they reproduce like rabbits, and the smell's not all that bad."

"Pigs should suit you very well, you bacon-brain!" Lucy spoke up from Johnny's lap, begad! "Love thy neighbor as thyself."

"What?" Kerry couldn't think. Johnny looked at him slantwise, then started to repeat his pig lecture.

Midway through, an exasperated Lucy shouted, "Hire him, you looby!"

A smile started to break across Lord Stanford's face. "Can you ride, John?"

"Well enough. I won't be doing any steeplechasing the way we used to, but I can get by."

The smile was now a grin, lighting Kerry's whole face. "Tell me, my friend, do you believe in heaven and hell?"

Norris shrugged. "Hell was Waterloo. Heaven is every day I'm alive."

So Kerry had a steward. And a secretary. According to Lucy, that clerk by the fireplace, Jeremiah Sidwell, had been dismissed from his recent position for reporting his superior's errors to their employer, who happened to be the superior's father. He was homeless, friendless, and a financial wizard. Just what a penniless earl needed.

Chapter Thirteen

$\mathcal{T}$he Earl of Stanford awoke in a better frame of mind in a too-short bed in a guest chamber, but at least the fireplace there worked. He threatened the butler and two footmen with instant dismissal if the chimney in his own room was not repaired by nightfall, he demanded an interview with his mother for that afternoon, and he sent a frigidly formal note to Goldy Flint via his new secretary, requesting an accounting. And all of this before his kippers and eggs. The earl was ready to greet John's brother Ralph at nine in the morning. In London he'd never be out of bed, sometimes not yet in bed.

He took a deep breath on his way to the stables. Yes, even his head was clear. What a relief it was just knowing Johnny was going to be there to help with decisions, Sidwell to handle the details, and Lucy to . . . well, be Lucy. He was used to her, kept peering around corners and sniffing the air for a hint of her presence.

Ralph Norris was thrilled with the idea of owning Stanford's hunters and was prepared to come down heavy for them. He'd even brought cash. The grooms paraded each of the horses out of the stable block and around the ring, and Ralph turned down only a chestnut gelding that had shown some swelling just that morning.

"Save that one for when you hunt with Westcott," he advised Kerry. "The man's hunt-crazy. That's the way to get to his girl."

"I'm not interested in getting to any—" Kerry began, but Ralph wasn't listening. He was staring at the bays, the perfectly matched, record-setting, bang-up-to-the-bits pair that drew the earl's rig.

"I've got to have them, Stanford. And the curricle. I promised the wife we'd go make a stir in London after the baby's born. We had to cut the honeymoon short. Morning sickness, don't you know," he said proudly, making sure the earl was aware he'd gotten his bride in her current interesting condition on their wedding night.

The bays were just what Ralph needed, he decided. The price he offered was hard for a badly dipped man to refuse, especially when Ralph hinted he mightn't take the hunters if he couldn't have the bays.

Kerry looked at his bays again, and then at all the grooms standing about with long faces as they watched their positions being sold off.

The earl could do some bargaining of his own. If he was going to see his horses go, he may as well see the end of some other mouths to feed. "I'll part with the bays, Ralph, on one condition: you take on the stable staff that I won't be needing. You'll require extra men now, and you'll have to have them bring the horses over anyway."

No amount of bargaining or blackmailing could get Ralph to make the mixed breed Lucky part of the deal. The untrained mutt kept jumping up on the earl, leaving stable-dirt footprints on Kerry's Hessians. The dog barking disturbed the horses and interfered with negotiations, and he chewed up Ralph's gloves when he put them down to write a bank draft for the curricle and pair.

"Take him now or I'll give him to your son as a christening gift," Kerry threatened, to no avail. At least Lucky wasn't as expensive as all those stablehands.

Ralph's check went to Sidwell for the bank; the cash went into Kerry's locked desk, not the vault whose combination was known to the countess.

"We'll decide on expenditures after Johnny and I make a more extensive survey of the estate, and after I hear from Gideon Flint." Kerry wasn't even trying to keep his personal affairs secret. Why should he bother in the house when the county knew? Furthermore, the man was already conversant with the earl's financial embarrassments, having gone halfway through the past five years' estate ledgers before breakfast. Kerry checked; they were indeed the same record books he could barely decipher.

There were still hours to go before luncheon—Kerry had never realized how long the day was when one met it before noon—so he decided to make the tour with Johnny, before taking on Lady Stanford. Leaving Sidwell happily making notations, Lord Stanford returned to the stables, pleased with the day's accomplishments.

Until he realized he'd left himself nothing to ride. Johnny was astride a sturdy, well-mannered gray, and grinning. The old head groom, who was staying on along with Lady Stanford's aged coach driver and two young boys, scratched his head. The gelding had poultices on its leg. The carriage horses were placid, plodding beasts who had never been ridden. And Aunt Clara's old mare was as old as Aunt Clara. If the pony from Cook's cart could bear Kerry's weight, his feet would touch the ground.

"There's a horse fair in Farley today," Johnny offered helpfully, still smiling. Kerry allowed as how it wasn't gentlemanly to knock a one-armed man off his horse.

The cash drawer was unlocked; Sidwell made more notations; Johnny would use the time to move his traps into Wilmott's cottage; and Aunt Clara's mare was saddled.

Lucy didn't even come keep the earl company on the long, slow, bumpy trip to Farley. Of course not. A curricle was exciting, fast, and flashy. A tired old nag was beneath Miss Faire's dignity. Now whose value system was suspect?

He'd be late for the interview with the dowager. Kerry was sure she wouldn't mind. He'd also be late for lunch by a few hours, so he bought himself a meat pasty to eat as he walked from paddock to paddock of the horse fair. In Farley at last, the earl vowed to walk home if he couldn't find a suitable mount. It would be quicker.

He needed a horse, but he needed money for hogs. Therefore he bypassed the front lines of horses on display, those he might have considered at Tattersalls. He also once considered a thousand pounds a reasonable price for a colt with potential. Those days were gone, so he tried not to look at the blooded cattle, the prime bits all curried and braided and prancing through their paces. The next ranks of horses were bound to suit his purse better, if not his taste. Meat pasties and someone's breakdowns, he reflected. How the mighty were fallen. Except he didn't feel diminished in the least; he felt more carefree than in years, almost boyish, dripping juice down his chin and planning to bargain like a rug merchant.

The problem was he couldn't find a horse worth considering. If the price didn't start too high, the horse was too old, too flashy, or too light for his weight. That one might be pretty in the park, but would tire under constant hard riding. This one was too excitable to be trustworthy anywhere outside a ring. One was a cribber, another was weak-chested, a third had a bad hitch.

Kerry did ask several grooms to put their horses through their paces, but none showed well. One rider even confessed his horse couldn't jump, when Kerry asked the lad to set him at a fence. Fine mount that one would be to get around land with fallen trees, streams, and hedges.

One horse did catch his eye, a chestnut mare with a white blaze. She had an intelligent look to her, and a nicely compact but graceful body. She just wasn't big enough for him. The mare would make a fine lady's mount, he judged. Too bad he wasn't in the market for one. Lucy would like how the mare came right over to have her ears scratched.

"Lookin' fer a nice ride fer yer wife, gov?" the eager horse coper asked, noting his interest. "T'mare's trained to sidesaddle, she is."

"Sorry, I'm not married."

"Yer sweetheart, then. Fine gent like you has to have a sweetheart. Yer lady friend would look an angel on this pretty horse."

Kerry answered, "My lady friend already is an angel," and walked on.

"That was lovely," Lucy told him, putting her arm through his.

The earl realized that patting an arm no one else could see must look ridiculous, but he did it anyway, hoping for the warm shiver her touch usually brought. "It was the truth."

"The angel part isn't, and you know it, but I meant how nice that you consider me a friend."

A comrade wasn't at all what the horse dealer had meant by lady friend, but Kerry didn't tell her so. He only repeated that of course they were friends.

Lucinda knew exactly what the trader meant; she simply chose to ignore it and be pleased by the earl's words. Smiling, she told him, "I am so glad. I have never had a friend before."

"What, never? Not in the village or at school?"

"My father did not consider the village children fit company for me, and he believed that too much education is bad for a woman, so I was taught at home. You are my first friend."

"Gads," he said, jaw clenched, "I'd like to give you back what you've missed, show you some of the world."

Lucinda only laughed. "I've seen more of the world in your company these past few days than any gently reared female sees in a lifetime! Gaming hells, bachelor quarters, taverns, bordellos, horse fairs. That's the real world, not balls and Venetian breakfasts." She waved her hand around. "This is the real adventure and, look, there are no other women."

That served only to remind him that she didn't belong in a rough place like this with men shouting who-knew-what back and forth across the aisles between makeshift stalls. Thank heaven none of the louts could see how charming she looked this morning, with a wide-brimmed bonnet trimmed with artificial cherries. There was even a lace overskirt to her gown, which was ridiculously out of place here amid the piles of manure.

The sooner he found a suitable mount, the sooner they could leave. Kerry approached the next row of horses with a less critical eye. He'd have to be blind to buy any of those, however.

Lucy must have wandered off while he studied a dappled gray that appeared passable, for she was back and trying desperately to get his attention over the surrounding noise while a groom led the gray around on a lead.

"Over here. Come on." She urged him on to the corner of the next row, where high fences had been put up around a grassy area. Men were sitting on the fence or leaning against it, yelling encouragement or derision to whatever was going on inside. When they got closer, Kerry could see that a door, brass knob and all, was propped against the fence. Rudely lettered on the door was the legend: STALLION FOR FREE IF YOU RIDE IT. 20s. A TRY.

"You can't mean me to wager on this swindle, Lucy. They find a horse that's unrideable, then make a fortune at these country fairs off the cabbageheads who are vain enough to try. Next day they move on to the next gathering of gullible gapeseeds. Half the fence-sitters are in on the hoax, making side bets about how long the rider stayed aboard, how many bones were broken. They even keep the door handy to carry away the casualties."

"Come closer, he's a real beauty."

The huge black stallion was magnificent except for the mud and blood on his sides, the sweating, heaving flanks, rolling eyes, laid-back ears, and flaring nostrils.

Kerry stepped back from his position along the fence. "Lucy, he looks like the meanest brute in creation. No one is going to ride that bonebreaker. It's a waste of coin to try."

"You could."

He laughed. "I thought we were friends. Thank you for the vote of confidence, but this time I'll pass." Kerry looked around at the crowd of men along the fence. "I see a lot of gamecocks corkbrained enough to try, but not one I'd lay my brass on."

"I don't want you to bet against the horse. I want you to buy him!"

"Perhaps you didn't understand the sign. You pay just to try. No one gets the horse, because no one rides him."

"Stop being so patronizing. Just because I cannot pick up a rock and throw it at you doesn't mean I cannot understand the King's English. *You* can ride the horse, therefore you can own the horse."

"Lucy, that is the most foul-tempered animal I

have ever seen. Why would I want to own him in the first place? I wouldn't wish that widow-maker on Gideon Flint. In the second place, I thought you wanted to keep me around for a few more days."

"He's mean only because the owner beats him. The poor thing is frightened half to death."

"Is that supposed to make me more eager to get in the ring with him? It doesn't."

"But when the owner can't find anyone else to try riding him, he'll kill the poor thing."

Her eyes were shining with unshed tears. He looked away. "That's what they do with man-hating horses, Lucy. It's the only solution."

"But he's one of God's creatures."

"So am I, and I don't want you shedding any tears over me, so I'll just keep looking for a nice horse that doesn't kill people for a living. Besides, this is gambling."

"Not if it's a sure thing, it isn't."

A sure thing, eh? Kerry walked around until he spotted the scurvy cur who seemed to be in charge.

"Had many take your challenge today?"

The man spat off to one side and jerked his head toward a bucket on the other. The bucket was almost filled with coins, most silver, some gold.

"That many fools, eh? And you still own the horse?"

The fellow spat again.

Kerry reached for his purse, then put his hand in his other pocket, the one with his lucky coin. "Do I get this back if I win?"

A tobacco-juice-dribbling nod was his reply.

"Then count in one more fool." Kerry tossed his coin into the bucket and asked, "What's the bastard's name anyway?"

"Hellraker."

"It figures."

When Kerry turned from draping his greatcoat over the fence, Lucy was in the pen with the great hulking beast, stroking his nose and whispering in his ear. The stallion seemed to be soothed somewhat, to his lordship's amazement.

"He can hear you and see you?" Kerry asked without fear of being overheard by the screaming gallery of oddsmakers and wagerers.

"I told you, he's frightened nearly to death, that's why. Now, go on, get up."

Kerry did, with the stallion's quivering acceptance. "Nice Hellraker, good Hellraker. Listen to Lucy, boy. We all do."

The black let Kerry walk him forward a few paces, Lucy's hand on the bridle.

"You gots to trot 'im twict 'round the ring, they's the rules," someone called from astride the fence.

Lucy started running, her hand still touching the horse. He trotted, at her speed, then faster, until her hand was just touching his rump. They all made one lap of the ring.

By then, however, under Lucy's tender influence, the stallion wasn't quite so scared of Kerry, not nearly frightened to death. So he didn't see Lucy floating along beside, or hear her soft voice whispering kindnesses into his ear.

"Oh, dear," she called as the stallion suddenly reared up on his back legs. "I'm afraid you're on your own."

"God damn you to h—" Kerry yelled as the back of Hellraker's neck collided with his nose at great force. The crowd thought he meant the horse. Lucy knew better. She disappeared. Kerry didn't notice, through the pain and the blood and the necessity to hang on to this monster with every ounce of strength he had. If he fell off, no doubt the beast would trample him and then he wouldn't live long enough to wring Lucy's neck. So what if she were already dead? He'd—

Out of the clear blue sky thunder suddenly rolled, a huge peal that meant a lightning storm was almost upon them. It wasn't as loud as the sound of Kerry's nose breaking, but it was a clap of thunder loud enough to put the fear of God into man . . . or scare a horse half to death.

ham of Casino Halso Spring that L.W. was thrown
flowing with rouge of her life will it God his
face the earn a horse that be home.

Chapter Fourteen

$\mathcal{T}$he dowager fainted when she saw her son. Kerry was not in prime twig for that confrontation but, oh, if he could get his hands on that harbinger of hell, Miss Lucinda Faire.

After the thunder she calmed the wild stallion enough for Kerry to complete the required circuits, get down, collect his gold piece and his greatcoat, and get back up. If he didn't remount then, Kerry knew, the beast would never let him, and he'd never have his mind so muddled that he'd try again. So he owned an incorrigible, unmanageable mountain of a horse. Now all he had to do was get it home. With Lucy gone, of course.

After tossing some coins to a lad to see the mare got back to the Abbey safely, he gestured to the disgruntled thimble-rigger to open the gate. The poltroon did, with a parting stream of tobacco juice for Kerry's boot and a farewell slash of his whip for the stallion.

Well, the earl didn't have to worry about the black taking fences or leaping fallen trees. The beast jumped gates, carts, and pedestrians, anything that got in his way. All Kerry had to concern himself with was wiping away the blood that still streamed down his face, keeping the horse pointed in the right direction, and staying in the saddle. And ridding his world—and afterworld—of the devil's handmaiden.

"'Vengeance is mine,' sayeth the Lord," she quoted, for it did not take a mind reader to know his thoughts.

Unfortunately, Kerry was in his bath at the time, in the guest chamber. The butler swore the fireplace in the master chamber was being serviced that very afternoon, but the earl could not wait. He was lying back in the tub, trying to soak the aches and pains away, with a cold towel on his nose. That's what the physician had recommended, after realigning the bones. *That* agony Kerry also laid at Lucy's door.

Unhappily for his resentment's sake, she was looking adorably contrite. Her hair was up in loose curls threaded through with ribbon, and her décolletage was enhanced by a scrap of pink lace that still allowed the shadow of cleavage to show through. Her cheeks were rosy without paint, her eyes downcast.

"Oh" was all she said, for it definitely didn't take a mind reader to know Kerry's thoughts this time either.

"Blast!" He grabbed the iced towel and applied it where it could do the most good. "What in blazes do you mean by coming upon a gentleman in his bath? Get out of here!" he raged, sending the two footmen and their cans of fresh hot water back to the kitchen.

"It's not as if I'm a flesh-and-blood female, you know," she started to say when he interrupted with, "Well, I am. Flesh and blood, that is, and I'll pray you to remember it next time you think of entering my bedchamber or entering my name in the lists for mortal combat." He grabbed up a nearby towel and used it as a shield while he struggled into his dressing gown, then headed barefoot down the hall to his own chamber and wardrobe. "And a real lady would look away," Kerry grumbled, forgetting all about his earlier goal of broadening the misplaced innocent's horizons.

Lucinda had no intention of missing a glimpse of a magnificent male body—heaven knew when she'd get another chance—but she did regret the bruises starting to discolor along his ribs. "I am sorry, you know, about Hellraker. Can you not 'forgive, that ye be forgiven'?"

"Only if you stop spouting chapter and verse at me. Hellraker is a superb animal," the earl added magnanimously, reaching for his brush and comb. "And the thunder was a splendid trick."

"Thunder? What thund—"

Then they heard the moaning. A soft, lowing sound seemed to echo in the room around them. "Ooo, ooo."

"What the—?" Kerry tightened the belt of his robe and picked up the fireplace poker. "My word, it must be Uncle Nigel."

Lucy ran after him as he circled the large chamber, looking for the ghost. "Kerry, Uncle Nigel isn't dead."

The noise seemed to be loudest near the hearth. The earl scraped his knee on the andiron, he spun around so fast. "Isn't dead?"

That's when the ball of soot fell through the chimney and landed on Kerry's bare toes.

When the dust and ashes settled, the ball was revealed as a small boy, blackened, scraped, burned, and bloody. And sobbing loudly.

Having as much experience with crying children as he had with flying carpets, Lord Stanford cursed. "Bloody hell." Then he opened the door to the corridor and shouted for help, loudly.

Three footmen, Cobb the butler, Sidwell, and two other soot-covered individuals, one large, one small, entered the earl's bedroom. The large one doffed his top hat and made a bow. "Sorry, milord. They didn't say as 'ow the room was occupied, just to rush. An' Dickie here, 'e's new. Don't know 'is way 'round a chimbley is all. We be almost done now."

He reached out an ash-encrusted hand for the boy, but Dickie darted away, between the butler's legs and out of the reach of the two footmen. He headed straight for the earl and threw his filthy arms around Lord Stanford's bare knees.

"Here now, none of that," said Cobb, gone pale under his powdered wig at the affront to his employer's dignity. He did not, however, reach to pry the grimy child loose. The master sweep did, but Dickie ran to the earl's other side and latched on there.

He looked up with tear-streaked cheeks and drenched blue eyes, and whimpered, "Help me, please, mister."

Oh, hell, Kerry thought, another one of God's—and Lucy's—creatures. Dickie even smelled like her, right through the earl's swollen nose. Kerry bent down to the child's level. "Help you do what, Dickie?"

"Help me get away from Sniddon, please, sir. I don't want to go back up there. It's hot and dark and scary. I want to go home to my mama." He buried his head in Kerry's robe and started sobbing again.

Sniddon, the sweep, made another grab for the boy, but Lord Stanford stopped him with a raised eyebrow. "The child seems to be burned and bleeding. Why is that?"

"It's 'cause 'e ain't learned 'is trade yet, my lord. I told you 'e was new. You don't see Lem 'ere"—the other cinder-dark bundle of rags—"cryin' for 'is ma."

Lem was shaking his head vehemently.

"Lem seems a bit older, perhaps readier for such work."

"An' perhaps 'e's gettin' too big for the job. We needs the little tykes, we does, if you swells want your chimbleys done right. Now, I'll just be takin' the lad, my lord, an' gettin' on with the work you 'ired me to do."

The butler was nodding, the footmen were nodding, and Lem stared at his bare, scarred feet. The earl made no move to detach the clinging arms.

" 'Ere now, my lord, gimme the boy. You got no call interferin' in my business. I got papers, all right an' tight, to say I bought 'im proper."

"It's illegal to buy children, Sniddon."

" 'Is services, I meant to say. Apprenticeship is legal, ain't it, my lord? Paid ten shillings for 'im, I did, to use 'im till 'e's growed."

"No, he didn't, mister," the little boy wailed. "I was stole by Gypsies and he bought me from them."

"Gammon. 'Is ma sold 'im to buy gin, is what."

"My mama would never do that! You're a liar! I want to go home!"

Kerry believed the child. He did not believe all the bruises on Dickie's bare arms and legs came from climbing chimneys. Even if they were, the boy was little more than a babe, five or six at most. With a deep sigh and the thought that this deed should get Lucy a lot closer to heaven, Kerry reached toward his dresser for a coin. His lucky coin. He tossed it to Sniddon, who bit down to check the gold content. "It's real, and worth twenty-one shillings. Now, take it and get out without another word or I'll call in the magistrate to investigate your so-called papers of apprenticeship."

Sniddon took the money and Lem and departed. The butler exited with a flea in his ear about getting machinery in to clean the chimneys next time, or dangling the multitudinous footmen by their heels with rags on ropes. "Anything but another infernal scene like this one," the earl insisted. Then he demanded a maid or someone to come take charge of the brat. It seemed there was no such creature at Stanford Abbey.

There was Mrs. Cobb, the housekeeper, but she was as starchy as his nibs in the wig, according to the footmen. She didn't consider filthy urchins to be in her province. Lady Stanford's abigail rode an even higher horse. Cook was in the middle of supper preparations, and whatever maids hadn't left on account of the ghosts had left on the earl's arrival.

"Your lordship's reputation, beggin' your pardon, my lord."

Kerry ran a hand through his hair and looked beseechingly in Sidwell's direction. "Sorry, my lord, I know only numbers. I'll, ah, list the guinea under housekeeping expenses, shall I? Or under charity?" And the secretary fled before he could be dragooned into nursemaiding a weeping tot.

Just when Kerry feared he'd have to bathe the child himself—drowning seemed the only way of dislodging the barnacle—his prayers were answered. A female voice filled the air with motherly warmth: "What's the meaning of this outrage, you sap-skulled booby? I have company coming for dinner tonight, so why is the chimney sweep leaving before all the rooms are done? And why are you covered in soot? You'll have to hurry to fix yourself up. You still look like death in a dressing gown."

"Thank you for your concern, Mother, but you'll have to excuse me. I don't think any amount of effort will make me presentable to company this evening."

"That's neither here nor there. The Westcotts are coming and bringing Felicia, apurpose to meet you, so you'd better be there. It would be the height of rudeness to disappoint them. And don't look daggers at me. Since you canceled the ball, someone has to look after your interests and make sure you meet the proper young females."

"And someone has to make sure there is no intimate family dinner where we might discuss the Stanford rubies."

"Fustian. There is nothing to discuss. But what, pray tell, is that piece of offal clinging to your leg? Get rid of it at once."

Kerry ruffled the boy's hair—his hand was already smudged—and asked, "Do you like dogs, Dickie?"

"Oh, yes, sir," Dickie answered, wiping his nose on his filthy shirttails, to the dowager's further disgust, and staring up at the earl with worship in his eyes.

"Then this, Mother, is Master Diccon, my new kenneler. Of course he commands only one dog at the moment, but we are starting small."

"And that way you won't miss me so much when my mama comes for me."

Finding Dickie's mama might be harder than finding the proverbial needle in the haystack, Kerry feared. The needle might want to be found; Dickie's mama might not if she had, indeed, traded the boy for Blue Ruin. Lord Stanford just smiled and said, "I'll share my mama with you until then," which effectively curtailed the dowager's incipient lecture on duty, dignity, and dressing for dinner.

So Lord Stanford took another bath, after scrubbing Diccon through three changes of hot water. The child had started bawling again when Kerry tried to hand him over to a footman, so it was easier to do the job himself. He was already besmirched, and something about the boy's tears caught at emotions he never knew he possessed. Washed, the boy's hair was blond and curly, reminding Kerry of the cherub in the oil painting he had held back from sale. For his sons. Yes, an heir mightn't be a terrible idea after all, especially if he was a trusting, adoring tad who thought you could shake hands with the man in the moon. Of course Kerry might prefer his son to have his own brown hair instead of this pale yellow. Then again, gold-glinting red was nice.

The infant cleaned up better than Kerry did. Soap and kitchen salve might work wonders on the boy's bruises; nothing was going to mend a bulbous scarlet snout in time for public viewing.

Aunt Clara came to the rescue then, having rummaged in the attics for long-outgrown nankeen shorts and jackets while Kerry introduced Dickie to his old tin soldiers and some picture books from the nursery.

Even bubble-headed Aunt Clara noticed what a fine, well-mannered boy he was, no street beggar or city foundling at all. After more questioning they discovered that his name was not Dickie either, it was Richard, Richard Browne. But Diccon was what his father called him, so that was all right. Mr. Browne's name was, of course, Papa. And Diccon knew precisely where he lived: in London, near the park. There were only a few thousand Browne families in London, all near some park or other, but one bit of information seemed hopeful: Diccon's father sometimes took him to work, at a furniture warehouse.

Sidwell was put on the case at once, to contact Stenross in London and Bow Street if necessary. Someone had to be looking for the boy. Diccon was convinced to go along with a footman to view Lucky in the stables. His new charge might be permitted to sleep in the nursery that night, if he promised to be good and release his death grip on the earl's leg.

Aunt Clara started weeping as she watched the boy solemnly take a footman's hand. "Nigel and I wanted a big family, not like your mother, who was relieved to have the heir first thing. We weren't married long enough. Oh, how I wish I could have had a son of his to remind me, even after he was gone." She was sobbing into the handkerchief Kerry hastily handed over.

"Uh, Aunt Clara, they never did find Uncle Nigel's body, did they?"

"No," she sniffled. "I had them bury his fishing gear instead. I insisted on a headstone, you see."

Kerry didn't see at all, but knew he had to wait for Lucy to find out any more. He hurried back to his room to finish his own toilette. She was there waiting, and glowing.

Her gown seemed more rose-colored than red, and her hair, which looked more gold than titian tonight, was held back with a silk rose. Mostly she was smiling a smile that warmed the whole room, just for him.

"What you did was magnificent, and without any prompting."

"Oh, it wasn't so much," he preened. "I couldn't have the nipper blubbering all over the place, could I?"

"You could have handed him back to the sweep. Or had him carted off to the workhouse."

"He's just a baby!"

"Oh, Kerry, you do have a conscience after all!" The kiss she placed on his cheek *almost* felt like a summer breeze. And it *almost* made his nose feel better.

"Don't worry about that, it will heal only a little crooked."

"Crooked? My nose is going to be crooked?"

"Well, I think it will make you better looking, not so intimidatingly perfect. And you know what they say about vanity."

"No, and I don't want to. I do want to know about Uncle Nigel. What do you mean, he's not dead?"

"I checked. He's very much alive and living in France."

"In France? For all these years? Without telling anyone?"

"There was a war on, you know."

"I suppose he could have been captured and been

a prisoner of war," the earl said doubtfully. "But why hasn't he come home now that the war is over?"

"Well, he wasn't exactly a prisoner of war. He was more a spy."

"Then the government should have made a special effort to get one of their own people out earlier than this!"

"That's just it," she said as the dinner gong rang. "He wasn't a spy for England."

Chapter Fifteen

$\mathcal{D}$inner was not the complete disaster Kerry expected. His attire this evening was not up to Weston's standards in fit or style, but it was acceptable for a country gathering. The deficiencies went unnoticed in light of his battered face, which the Westcotts were too well bred to comment upon. Only John Norris grinned, until Kerry invited him to trade his cob for the black. Then Lord Westcott had to be shown the fearsome beast, so dinner was delayed for a trip to the stable, where Diccon was still playing with Lucky. The marquis was inclined to be suspicious of the boy's presence in a known libertine's household, but he was impressed with the horse despite himself.

"I wouldn't have gotten on his back for anything, not even in my salad days. Tossed salad, I'd be. I daresay a broken nose is a small price to pay for such a noble animal."

And Lord Westcott was off in a rambling, one-sided discourse of all the mean, unbroken horses he'd ever encountered. His monologue lasted through the soup course, the fish, meat, poultry, and sweets, with removes, and was directed to the entire table, not just his partner, the dowager. Lady Stanford kept a smile fixed on her face and pointedly fingered her paste diamonds whenever Kerry looked down the table in her direction. As if he needed a reminder that Westcott was as rich as Golden Ball, and had just the one chick.

Miss Felicia Westcott was a pretty girl, fair-haired, soft-spoken, elegantly dressed in a demure white gown with pearls at her neck and laced through her hair. Kerry thought he might have danced with her at some ball or other but he couldn't be sure; all debutantes tended to look alike. She blushingly denied it when he asked if they'd been introduced, so he gathered she'd been warned off rakes like him. But her duke hadn't come up to scratch, so the Earl of Stanford did not seem quite so reprehensible.

Well, marrying an heiress didn't seem quite so outrageous now either. Kerry vowed to keep an open mind.

Still, he was in no hurry to join the ladies after dinner, even though Lord Westcott's cigar made his hands shake with wanting a cigarillo. He sipped his port instead, and asked Johnny about his day appraising the lands for hog farming.

At the mention of hogs, Lord Westcott set off on a whole new saga of unruly beasts, culminating in the boar that had just trampled poor Tige Welford, one of his tenants. The widow was wanting to up and leave as soon as she could find someone to buy out her herd of pigs. Except for the boar. She'd shot the bastard and was even now making sausages. Westcott thought Kerry could get a deuced good bargain if he hurried. On the pigs, not the sausages.

Johnny was thrilled, even Kerry was excited. Sidwell was more cautious when consulted, citing the other costs involved. They carried the conversation and their glasses into the drawing room, where Miss Westcott was posed gracefully at the pianoforte. The marquis took a seat in the corner and placed a handkerchief over his face for a nap. Aunt Clara was sewing by the fire, and the two other ladies were enjoying shredding reputations on the sofa. Kerry directed John to turn Felicia's pages, so he could continue the discussion with Sidwell of how much of the horse sale money they could afford to pay out, after the secretary's study of the estate's income and expenses. Kerry did notice that Miss Westcott played adequately, more or less in keeping with Herr Beethoven's intentions, and softly enough not to impede conversation around her.

All in all, he congratulated himself after, it was a satisfactory evening. Of course he'd had to accept Lord Westcott's invitation to a hunt two days hence; that was the least he could do in recompense for the tip about Widow Welford's pigs. Lord Westcott declared he wanted to see the black in action. Kerry didn't need Johnny's wink and his mother's satisfied smirk to know the marquis actually wanted to see his prospective son-in-law in action.

"Tell me again about Uncle Nigel, Lucy. I don't know why I'm having such a hard time accepting it. After all, if I can think nothing of having a comfortable coze with a soul in transit, I should not cavil at Uncle Nigel's being a spy."

Kerry was sitting in front of the fireplace in his own room, sipping a cognac. Lucy was sitting across from him with her embroidery, but the mirror over the mantel showed a solitary gentleman in his robe and slippers, talking to an empty chair.

Lucy set aside the altar cloth and smiled. "He never wanted to be, you know."

"I didn't suppose anyone ever wanted to be a spy. I mean, it's not as if some boys are mad to enlist in the army, others hear a calling to join the clergy, and Uncle Nigel grew up itching to be a traitor to his country. All Nigel wanted to do, as far as I ever heard, was go fishing."

"And so he did that day, but his boat capsized. While he was hanging on, waiting for rescue, a fishing ketch came along. Only it wasn't really a fishing boat, and the sailors were not English. They gave him the choice: stay there or come with them back to France. They would not return him to the English shore for fear of the patrols. He might have been rescued, but his arms were getting tired, and the water was getting cold. So he accepted their offer."

"Understandable. He was just saving his own skin."

"Yes, but then the smugglers felt he owed them something for their trouble, so he helped them unload their cargo."

"Which was?"

"Guns."

"Which was treason."

"Exactly. And they said they'd kill him if he didn't tell them everything he knew."

"About what, for pity's sake? Uncle Nigel wasn't with the government or anything. He was just a gentleman of modest means who liked to fish."

"And who knew every current and tide and shoal on the coast of England and half of Scotland."

"Fiend seize it, so he did. And he told them?"

She shrugged. "He did not want to die. After he told them what they wanted, the French let him go to find his own way home. Ashamed of what he'd done, he thought he'd skulk around and discover their plans, to report back to the British."

"To prove his loyalty."

"Precisely. Instead, he got shot."

"But not killed?"

"No, he was taken in and nursed by a family of peasants who made a living fishing. As soon as he was recovered, he intended to pretend to be one of them, to earn passage home on another smuggling boat. Except . . ."

"Except?" Kerry was grinning now. Uncle Nigel's saga was starting to sound like a Minerva Press novel.

"Except that while he was unconscious, the patriarch of the family had him wed to one of the granddaughters. Nicolette was increasing, with decreasing chance of her *chère ami* coming forward."

"The marriage wasn't legal. He was already married, for one, unwilling for another."

"And not Catholic for a third. The family did not care. And Nicolette begged him to stay until the baby was born. What could he do? He had no money, these people had saved his life, and he had no state secrets to bring back to British intelligence anyway. The English would hang him, the French would shoot him. And Nicolette's father would skin him alive if he tried to escape."

"So he stayed all these years?" Kerry finished off his drink and sat up. "What about Aunt Clara?"

"He thought she could never forgive him, so he might as well stay away and let her get on with her life, remarry, have the family they wanted."

"Poor Aunt Clara."

"And poor Uncle Nigel. He wants so badly to come home to her—Nicolette has been dead for years—now that the war is over, but cannot afford to."

"Dash it, I can scrape passage money together. I can pawn my watch again, or Mother's paste diamonds."

"For two thousand pounds?"

Kerry sank back. "What, is he planning on buying a yacht to bring him across the Channel? Won't the packet boat do?"

"He cannot come home without a pardon. Living in France all those years, aiding the enemy . . ."

"With a few tide tables?"

"He also did some interpreting of smuggled papers, to earn extra money for the children."

"The children? No, don't tell me. This pardon thing, one doesn't just petition for it? We can get character witnesses, explain away the whole bumblebroth."

"In a perfect world, yes," she said with a frown. "In this one it requires bribes. Support for the Crown, I believe they call it." She took up her needlework again, angrily stabbing the needle through the fabric.

"Two thousand pounds." Kerry dropped his head back against the cushions. "Where the bloody hell am I going to get two thousand pounds? I already told Johnny we could use most of the horse sale money to buy the hogs, so there'll be an income down the road. And Sidwell thinks that if we chop down the home woods timber, we can earn enough to make the improvements necessary to get the tenants back, hence the rents. But that's years away. I even informed the countess that I couldn't pay a farthing toward her gaming debts. She fainted again, incidentally, when I told her that Flint can wear her diamonds on his next smuggling raid for all I care, but if he tries to sell the Stanford rubies, I'll have the both of them arrested. If I cannot afford to retrieve the engagement ring, I cannot afford to retrieve Uncle Nigel."

"So you liked Miss Westcott?" Lucy asked with feigned indifference.

"She's a pleasant enough chit. But that wasn't what I meant."

"She liked you." Lucinda sucked on the finger she pricked.

"She liked Johnny and Sidwell, too. Did you see the priceless look on Mother's face when I announced I'd invited my secretary and my steward to dinner? That alone was worth all the insipid chit chat. Evened the numbers at table, at any rate, and gave Miss Westcott her choice of gentlemen to flirt with. Of course Johnny stared at her like a moon-calf all night, and Sidwell stammered, but Felicia was happy."

"You didn't stare or stutter, yet she appeared pleased with your company." And why not? Lucinda asked, but kept the thought to herself. "So she might welcome your addresses. Then a match there mightn't be a simple financial arrangement, her money for your title."

"Now you're sounding like Aunt Clara, who looks for April and May everywhere. Everywhere but France, of course. No, I was not struck all aheap by Miss Westcott, and I doubt she is ready to throw her bonnet over the windmill for an earl residing in Queer Street."

"But if you could find pleasure in her company, and she in yours, then love could follow duty." Lucy ripped out the line of stitches she'd just sewn and bundled the cloth away.

"I doubt Miss Westcott has two thoughts to rub together beyond her clothes and her entertainments," he noted, holding his still-full glass of cognac toward the fire, watching the colors change. "Oh, and her horses."

Lucinda tilted her head to one side, studying his face. The only change she could see was the swollen nose and a healthier color. "But that's all you were interested in just a few days ago."

"Was it just this week? I feel I've known you forever." He laughed. "And is this effort to promote a match with Miss Westcott another thread in your fabric of my reformation? I thought we were doing well enough with saving fallen sparrows. Must you aim for leg shackles, too?"

"I wish to see you a better man, yes. But I like you, Kieren Somerfield. I also want to see you happy."

"Thank you. That means more to me than a hundred flirtatious simpers or batted eyelashes from the likes of Felicia Westcott. I like you, too, Miss Lucinda Faire."

They sat in comfortable silence broken only by the hiss of the dying fire, each deep in his or her own thoughts. Then Lord Stanford cleared his throat. "Ah, Lucy, if Uncle Nigel is alive in France, who the devil is Aunt Clara talking to?"

Chapter Sixteen

$\mathscr{D}$awn was not the best time for exercising horses—unless you wanted to make sure no one saw you make a cake of yourself falling off. Then again, it might be hours before anyone thought to look for his bruised and bloodied body. Kerry rather preferred it that way.

He'd prefer not to face Hellraker at all. His body was not in shape for another explosive battle of wills, and might never be. The horse would only grow more unmanageable left unridden, though, standing in a stall all day. It was better to school him again now, while he remembered yesterday's lessons.

Hellraker remembered, all right. He laid his ears back and ripped off a piece of the earl's jacket. He kicked and bucked and reared, but he got ridden to the point of exhaustion. The stallion learned—for the day at least—that he couldn't loosen Kerry from his back no matter what tricks he used. He also learned he wasn't getting whipped or raked with rowels at every turn. There was no blind obedience yet, but a little respect.

The respect went both ways. Lord Stanford came to appreciate the black's strength and stamina, and his courage, too. There was no hedge so high the stallion wouldn't take it flying, no stream so wide he didn't soar over. With a little more practice, the brute could make a fortune at every steeplechasing event in the county, if Kerry were a betting man, of course. He wasn't, not right now. Those cross-country events took a high toll on horses anyway, he consoled himself. 'Twould be a shame to have such a superior animal lamed.

Or maybe not, Kerry thought as he lost the rest of his sleeve rubbing the beast down. The real shame was that he'd let go all those stablehands. His head groom was too old to dodge the flying hoofs, and the younger lads were far too green. The only one the stallion seemed to tolerate, aside from his lordship, was the fool dog Lucky.

"Just make sure Diccon doesn't get too close," the earl instructed. Lud, what would happen if the boy followed the pup into Hellraker's stall? Had he ordered enough servants to watch out for the boy's welfare? Aunt Clara said she'd have breakfast with Diccon in the nursery, but what then? Gads, a child was a headache. If the Brownes weren't located soon, Kerry supposed he'd have to hire a nurse-maid, then a governess, tutors. After that would come a school or a trade. In the meantime were clothes and books and toys and food. Enough food for a growing boy's appetite could bankrupt him. Zeus, when he remembered his own schooldays, he wondered if even the new pigs would be safe.

Which reminded him that he was going to need a boar soon, if he wished to stay in the hog business. All this worrying about money made him feel crass, mercenary. Dash it, things were easier in the old days, when fortunes were won or lost on the turn of a card.

Johnny Norris was back from Welford's farm with good news about the pig deal. They were ready to be fetched as soon as Stanford Abbey was ready for them. Unless they were to be lodged in the east wing, where the roof still leaked, the home woods had to go.

"But not the whole of it," Johnny contended. "I never thought much of that clear-cutting. We could just take what we need in the old growth, let the young trees get more sun. That way you keep the rabbits and quail and deer, and have more timber to cut in a few years' time."

"That sounds too reasonable. Why doesn't everyone else do it that way instead of clearing the whole stand and planting over it?"

"It's harder," Johnny admitted. "Takes more manpower, and you get less yield all at once. But long-range . . ."

So Kerry lined up all those useless footmen, everyone but Simpson, who had a knack with neckcloths, Jeffers, who had Diccon riding on his shoulders, and Derek, who lisped.

"I don't need my silver polished to a fare-thee-well, nor my rugs beaten to a pulp," he told the assembled servants. "I need pens and troughs and sheds, and fields ready to be planted come spring in pig fodder. I need drainage ditches dug, roof tiles replaced, roads graded. I'll understand if you wish to stay as footmen in your warm jobs and clean livery, but you can't stay here. I cannot support you, not with all the additional men I'll need. You'll get references and your pay. If you decide to stay on, there will be a rotating schedule of housework and field jobs, and I promise a return to your usual positions as soon as circumstances permit."

Most of the footmen accepted, knowing how few jobs there were these days, and so did the young grooms, the tenants who were behind in the rents, and whatever out-of-work villagers Johnny could find. With a few experienced lumbermen hired on from Farley, the Earl of Stanford and his crew sallied forth.

In no time at all, fence posts were being cut, and fingers. Shed poles were being raised, and blisters. Shovels, axes, and saws were being employed, and muscles long unused to such hard physical labor. The Earl of Stanford was right there with the men, digging holes and splitting wood or loading fallen trees onto wagons for the lumber mill.

Sweaty and sore, his clothes in muddy tatters, his only pair of boots scored and scraped, the once-fastidious earl was thinking that an heiress mightn't be such a bad thing. Which was a good thing, for Sidwell came out to tell him that Lady Prudlow and her granddaughters had arrived for tea.

He tried, he really did. He made polite conversation, he made insincere compliments. With a Prudlow sister on either arm, he made a tour of the portrait gallery. They giggled and tittered; he shut his ears. For all his attempts to kindle a spark of interest in his own breast, the earl kept wishing he was back in the fields with the men. For all his sipping catlap and nibbling macaroons, he couldn't even tell which Prudlow chit was Priscilla, which Patricia. At least Miss Westcott had a bit of presence.

Just as he was wishing the sisters and their garrulous grandmother to Jericho, Cobb the butler came into the drawing room, his wig askew. It seemed there was a commotion of some sort in the hallway, and without the legions of footmen, he was forced to handle things himself. Could his lordship be so kind as to step outside a moment?

Kerry went, followed by his curious female relatives and their even more rudely inquisitive guests. Derek, the footman who lisped, was trying to deal with box after box being unloaded from a hired carriage that was drawn up at the front door. Diccon was underfoot, for his temporary nanny, Jeffers, was outside doing the unloading, and Lucky was

141

barking. Simpson, the footman elevated to valet just that morning, had taken one look at the names on the boxes—Weston, Stultz, Hobbes—and had gone to join the men in the fields.

"What the—?" Kerry recognized the formal tailcoat he'd ordered before leaving town, but these carefully folded shirts, waistcoats, and breeches couldn't be the clothes Demby was to have cleaned and sent on if the smell of smoke came out. Kerry's whole wardrobe could have been contained in a small trunk, not this mountain of apparel in boxes bearing the names of London's best outfitters.

"There is a letter, my lord." Cobb held out a silver salver.

"Will you excuse me, ladies?" Kerry asked, hinting the women back into the drawing room to continue their tea. "Perhaps Diccon could have a raspberry tart, Aunt Clara?" No one left, and Diccon continued chasing Lucky through the piles of parcels, trying to get a brand-new York tan glove out of the pup's mouth. The Prudlow sisters giggled while their grandmother surveyed the scene through her pince-nez. Aunt Clara was admiring one particularly fancy waistcoat embroidered with forget-me-nots, and Lady Stanford was fuming.

"You can't afford a few piddling gaming debts, eh?" she hissed in his ear, punctuating her remarks with a jab to his midsection. "A ball is too expensive, eh?" Another jab. "You can't finance an adequate household staff, what? But you can rig yourself out like a caper merchant, is that it?"

Kerry stepped aside before she punctured his abdomen. "I swear I had nothing to do with this. If I may be permitted to read the note?"

She didn't give permission; he withdrew to the steps and read anyway.

Demby—for the note was indeed from the earl's former valet, groom, et cetera—wrote about winning the firemen's benevolent raffle lottery, which Kerry already knew. He was sorry, but he would not be returning to the earl's service, which Kerry also knew. Demby was buying a partnership in a small foundry, where he hoped to set up a studio and shop, to work on his sculpture. This was not very surprising, considering the man's revelations on the night of the fire. What was amazing to his lordship was Demby's next line, that he wished to share some of his windfall with his former employer. Not only had Lord Stanford given him the winning ticket, Demby wrote, and saved his life to boot, but the earl had also given him employment where he was free to practice his art. (No mention was made of Demby's feigned tremors, nor the fact that the job was practically a volunteer position in recent times.)

In return, Demby wished to show his appreciation. But how? He knew his lordship's casual attitude toward money, that the earl would lose whatever Demby sent before the ink was dry on the check. He was taking the liberty, therefore, of sending along those recently ordered replacement items for Lord Stanford's wardrobe, and a few additions.

Kerry looked around. Those few additions included enough satin knee breeches to clothe an Almack's gathering, enough lace and linen cravats to strangle the House of Lords, and enough beaver hats to cause extinction of the species. Nightshirts, stockings, dancing slippers, nothing was overlooked—except sturdy boots, woolen shirts, heavy fustian trousers, and a frieze coat for carrying hogmash.

Sitting down on the marble steps amid all that splendor, Kerry threw his head back and laughed. The roof was literally falling down around his head, he hardly had a pot to put his pigs in, debts were piled atop obligations, and he'd be dressed better than Beau Brummell. He laughed even harder when Diccon and Lucky knocked over a box containing a stack of silk drawers. He held one pair aloft, sending all three Prudlow ladies scurrying for the door, and gasped, "And they said you couldn't make a silk purse out of a sow's earl!"

When he finished wiping his eyes, the hallway was empty of everyone but Lucy, who was shaking her finger reprovingly. "That was not well done of your lordship." But her lips twitched. "If there was anyone in the neighborhood who hadn't heard you had a draft in the rafters, they'll be informed by nightfall. And those were nice girls you just chased away!"

"They were ninnyhammers, and you know it. Why, marriage to a peahen like that would send me hieing back to London and one expensive mistress after another, so where would be the benefit? Not in morals, not in the pocketbook. Be content for now, I'll be the best-dressed pig farmer in Wiltshire."

"Just don't go getting puffed up with your own conceit again," she warned. "Your nose hasn't healed yet."

The earl went to bed early that night, throwing out his new valet, lisp and all, before Derek was through the unpacking. Kerry'd been up since dawn at hard physical labor, and had to face Lord Westcott, his hunt, and Hellraker in the morning. Mostly, though, he was hoping Lucy would come again. He was eager to see if his hard day's work met with her approval, if there'd been any change in her appearance to match his blisters and scrapes.

He laughed at himself, inventing excuses to look at Lucy. Why, he hardly took his eyes off her when she was in the room. She fascinated him, he admitted, all innocence and passion combined. He'd never known a woman like her, and not just because she was a specter. If he had to choose a wife, that was the type of woman he wanted, halfway between devil and angel, not some milk-and-water miss like the Prudlow girls. They could never hold a candle to Lucy anyway. A man wouldn't get bored with a female like Lucinda Faire, with her challenging mind and caring nature. And honesty. Why, no woman had ever said she liked him before. There was flattery aplenty, and protestations of undying love, especially outside the jewelry shops, but never simple, honest liking. A man could even trust a female like that, as opposed to a Miss Westcott, whose motives must ever be suspect.

Lucy was a *real* woman. No, blast it, she wasn't a real woman at all. If he tried to touch her, his hands would go right through. If he tried to hold her, call her, keep her, she just danced through his dreams the way she drifted through his life, turning everything upside down.

And he needed a woman, especially after thinking of Lucy, even if he did not need a wife. Celibacy was not Kerry's strong point, nor a virtue he saw much point in pursuing, except that *she* was sure to appear then, and not now, when he wanted her company. Lucy would be steaming mad, singeing him—if not his privates—with her scorn.

The thought did much toward cooling his ardor. Perhaps he could live without a woman's services for a while after all, especially if he had Lucy's lively conversation and luscious form to admire.

She never came.

Kerry rolled over and went to sleep, thinking the hell with her. And dreamed of her anyway.

Chapter Seventeen

If clothes made the man, Kieren Somerfield was the warlord of Wiltshire, the hero of the hunt. His scarlet jacket was a marvel of tailoring, allowing supple movement while defining his broad shoulders and narrow waist. The doeskin breeches fit like a second skin, and the white high-topped boots gleamed with a champagne polish. Demby had outdone himself, with Derek's help. The earl was splendid, except for the vivid colors around his nose that rivaled the scarlet jacket in brilliance.

If the mount made the rider, however, Kieren Somerfield belonged on the wooden rocking horse in the nursery. Hellraker did not appreciate the yowling hounds, the blaring trumpet, or standing around in Westcott Hall's carriage drive, waiting for the rest of the hunt to assemble. In ten minutes Kerry's cravat was disordered, his hair was disheveled, and his hat was missing altogether.

Going on the hunt had not been a good idea. Polite and politic, but not clever. Hellraker was untested, not ready for public exhibition. The men at the Abbey would get less accomplished without the earl, despite Johnny's supervision. Diccon kept crying, sure the Gypsies would come snatch him away while his idol was off riding. And the grapevine had it that Goldy Flint had returned from whatever nefarious mission he'd gone on.

Mostly, however, Kerry's attendance at the hunt was a poor notion because of Lucy. He should have known the fox would be one of those of God's creatures requiring Miss Faire's attentions. He kicked himself for not thinking, saving Hellraker the effort.

By George, chickens were God's creatures, too, and He didn't seem too concerned about losing a few of those to Reynard. And why the deuce couldn't God just save the mangy beast Himself, Kerry wondered, without involving him? A good drenching rain would hide the scent and cancel the hunt. For that matter, why didn't the earth open up and swallow the blasted vermin, saving them all the effort? Most likely, he reasoned, because Lucy wanted him to get the dubious credit. Of course she didn't care what his neighbors thought, as long as he looked good to the Weird Sisters who would seal his fate.

So there was Lucy, two rises over, on hands and knees, trying to unstop the burrow so the fox could go to ground. Tarnation! Kerry was already having enough trouble keeping Hellraker well back from the leading riders so he did not outrun the hounds. Miss Westcott had stayed behind to check his condition, making polite conversation and keen observations on his handling of the obstreperous stallion. He waved her on, indicating a need to check his saddle girth.

When the last rider ambled by, Kerry directed Hellraker toward the hill where Lucy was still trying her best to make dirt move. The flurry of dust indicated her frenzy. She wasn't getting very far very fast.

He got down, holding tightly to Hellraker's bridle. "The hunt is well away in the other direction, Lucy. The fox mightn't come back this way at all."

She gave him a look of scorn. "And Demby's lottery ticket might have lost, too. Now, are you going to help?"

There went his beautiful new riding gloves, and a piece of his breeches—and backside—that Hellraker made a swipe at. And all for naught, for sure enough, Kerry could see the fox come streaking across the field in their direction too soon. The hunt was still out of sight, but the hounds would be on the scent.

"Do something!" Lucy demanded.

"Like what?" he shouted back.

"Pick him up and take him away!"

Pick up a fox? Take him away? She was daft, besides dead. Yet there she was, lifting the small red creature and handing him over, with a beseeching look.

"He has only ten minutes to live, that's how he came to me."

The fox knew damned well that Kerry wasn't any angel or anything, and struggled. "Take him!" Lucy cried, just ahead of the first baying of hounds.

Kerry took the wriggling beast. He opened his lovely scarlet coat and buttoned the fox inside, then remounted. Just as the hunt master came into view, Kerry made Hellraker rear to show he was having trouble with his mount, explaining why he was riding off in the opposite direction. It was an easy enough trick, getting the stallion to act like an unbroken colt, but it also caused the fox to do what many a young, frightened animal will do.

Kerry vowed he'd kill that female if it was the last thing he did. Hell couldn't be worse than this, the dampness seeping right through his waistcoat to his lawn shirt and down his breeches, his neck-or-nothing neighbors laughing at him, and a pack of slavering hounds hot on his heels. Whatever he did, he couldn't stay here.

Thinking quickly, Kerry circled around and raced back toward the end of the field of riders, where the last stragglers, the vicar and a few boys too young to be at the hunt were dawdling along. He figured the hounds would lose the scent with the prey above their heads. He and Hellraker must be carrying so much *eau de* fox, though, that soon the pack was turning, chasing its own tail as it were. So much for that plan.

Kerry left the vicar's company when they reached a stream. The overweight cleric's slug of a horse rightfully refused to exert himself enough to get them both over the water, which Hellraker cleared without a splash. Too bad the hounds wouldn't be confused by the broken trail. They'd pick up the fox on the other side in minutes, the stream being so narrow. The stream was quite long, however.

Unfortunately Hellraker disagreed with the new strategy of wading upstream far enough that the hounds would be thrown off the scent. In addition to being ridden, it appeared, Hellraker also had an aversion to getting his feet wet. There was nothing to do but for Kerry to dismount, still holding the quivering fox against his chest, and lead—drag— Hellraker over the rocks and rivulets.

Leaving the stream when his own toes were turning numb from the cold water getting into his boots, Kerry started to unbutton his coat.

"Don't put him down!" Lucy shrieked. "They decided to end the hunt, so they are going home this way!"

"Blast it, what am I supposed to do? Bad enough they'll think I took a header into the stream, but riding back to nuncheon with a fox in my pocket? Lucy, it's only a—"

"Put him up a tree. They don't have the scent yet. If he's high enough, the dogs won't pick up his smell." She wrinkled her nose. "Likely they'll follow you again anyway."

"Foxes can't climb trees, Lucy!"

"But you can. Please?"

"And how will he get down again after I lead the hunt away, or haven't you thought of that, Mistress Mayhem?"

"Why, you'll come back and put him down later, of course, while they're having lunch."

Climbing a tree with one hand, in wet boots, with a ghostly female shouting encouragement, did nothing for Kerry's temper. Neither did the scrapes along his cheeks from the tree bark, the scratches on his hands from the ungrateful fox, the flapping fabric on his breeches, or the disdainful look on Miss Westcott's face as she rode by him, not a hair out of place, not a speck of mud on her velvet riding habit. Missing luncheon with the arrogant chit was the only ray of sunshine on a gray, gray day.

In a new suit of clothes but the same frame of mind, Lord Stanford set out for Mr. Gideon Flint's house that afternoon. The same starched-up butler informed the earl that he would have passed Mr. Flint on the road if he hadn't come cross-country, a reference to the muddy bite-marks on Kerry's boots and the limpness of his cravat. Hellraker's mood hadn't improved either. Mr. Flint, the butler deigned to disclose, was out paying afternoon calls. Stanford Abbey was certain to be on his itinerary. It usually was.

Curses! Kerry had forgotten to leave instructions barring the door to Mr. Flint. He could be at the Abbey that very moment, chousing the dowager out of the pictures in the portrait gallery, or the sterling silver tea set. Conversely, Kerry still needed to talk to the old makebait to find out his price for the rubies, not that he needed the betrothal ring in any hurry, although Miss Westcott had managed to show some sympathy at the end of the hunt. Everybody had their good days and their bad days, she'd commiserated, and today was the fox's good day. She'd never know. Meanwhile Kerry watched her blue eyes shift over his various stains and spatters, mentally counting to herself how many times he and Hellraker must have parted company. Still, she was polite about his refusal to lunch, poised in the face of his dishabille, and a bruising rider. He could do worse, like one of the Prudlow twits.

Flint had come and gone at the Abbey by the time Kerry checked on the progress of the hog pens. The dowager was resting and had her maid refuse the earl entry—and a chance to relieve his ire. Not till dinner did he get the opportunity to discuss Free-trader Flint, and that in front of Aunt Clara, Johnny Norris, and Sidwell. Therefore, Kerry could not exactly express himself in the terms he might have chosen, terms like *gallows-bait* and *over my dead body*. Instead, he was forced to inquire when Mr. Flint might next honor them with his presence.

"Oh, you'll see him at the assembly two nights hence," the dowager replied. "Over at Farley. Since we will not be holding a ball, I decided we should attend so that you'll meet the neighbors. Miss Westcott and the Prudlows will be expecting you to dance with them."

Kerry attacked his turbot in oyster sauce with unnecessary vigor. "They will be disappointed."

"Don't be churlish, Kieren. Of course you are going. I accepted for all of us." She glared around the table as if daring anyone else to disagree with her. Johnny and Sidwell applied themselves to their meal with renewed diligence. "And Mr. Flint made special mention that he hoped to discuss a certain topic with you," she said with arched brows.

"Oh, it's to be one of those democratic country affairs where they allow in anyone with the price of admission? How quaint. Shall I dance with the butcher's daughter also, Mother? Perhaps I should consider one of the dairy maids for next countess."

"Have I told you recently how much you remind me of your father?"

Kerry swallowed a forkful of veal. "Thank you, ma'am."

"That was no compliment, you clunch. And we shall not be attending a village barn dance, contrary to your priggish comments, but an exclusive gathering of the best of local society."

"With Goldy Flint?"

"Mr. Flint is hosting the affair."

Aunt Clara would not go, she declared with a sneer for her sister-in-law. It wasn't fitting for a widow in mourning.

"After twenty years? Besides, you hypocrite, you've gone to balls and routs and picnics anytime you've been invited. If you had the sense God gave a duck, you'd leave off those wretched weeds and find yourself a new husband instead of living in Kieren's pockets and talking to ghosts."

"Hah! A new husband like that . . . that . . ."

"Excuse me, my lord." Cobb interrupted what promised to be a scene unconducive to digestion. To Kerry's relief, there seemed to be another Situation in the hall. The butler's flaring nostrils eloquently expressed his disapproval of yet another episode beneath the dignity of the noble house he served.

"A Mr. and Mrs. Browne have arrived from London. They regret their advent during the dinner hour, but have been traveling since yesterday afternoon, it seems, in some high state of excitement, and beg your lordship's indulgence," Cobb recited. Then he added, "What shall I do with them?"

"Do with them, you clodpole? Find their son! What did you think, they drove all this way, through the night, too, just to interrupt my supper? How could you make them wait, man?" Kerry demanded to everyone's surprise. "Don't you have a heart?"

They should have let the Brownes hold their reunion in private, but Diccon came tearing down the stairs before Kerry could escort the blond young man and his frail-looking wife to a smaller private parlor. Soon there wasn't a dry eye in the Abbey, including the dowager's, who insisted the fireplace was putting out too much smoke.

Later, after Kerry refused to permit the Brownes to seek an inn for the night, he and Diccon's father shared a brandy in the library. Browne tried again to express his gratitude, and the earl again brushed his thanks aside. "Anyone would have done the same."

"No, my lord, they would not have. That's how such vile practices get perpetuated. There aren't enough men like you who are willing to take action." The younger man cleared his throat. "And I want to show my appreciation. I know better than to offer a gentleman like yourself the reward money, but it was substantial. My family owns one of the largest furniture factories in London. I had heard about the fire in your London home, and your visit to the showrooms of several of my associates. Mr. Stenross senior mentioned you might be bringing a bride home, so with the approval of Mr. Stenross junior, my family and friends have arranged delivery of those items you were considering, and a few additions."

Numbly, Kerry could only consider that the Stenross partners, like Demby, would not trust him with cash either.

A gentleman like himself could not ask the price of the furnishings, but the list Mr. Browne left for his perusal seemed to indicate that the reward money might have retiled the Abbey's leaking roof with gold leaf! If he weren't a grown man, Kerry would have wept.

London was waiting for him. His home and his person outfitted in splendor rivaling Prinny's, he merely had to sell that last painting to live the life he was used to, the life he understood. Who knew, he might even start attending Almack's and find himself a town-bred beauty with a princely portion.

Instead, here he was in Wiltshire, blistered, bilious, and broken-nosed, with his lovely clothes being used as horse fodder.

"Then why don't you leave?" Lucy asked. She appeared soft in the candlelight, and sad.

"Because you gave me a challenge, to bring this place up to snuff, and a Somerfield never backs down from a dare. I won't quit till it's done. As soon as the Abbey is in order, I'll shake the dirt of this place off my feet and be gone, so don't go thinking this is a permanent change in my lifestyle, for it isn't."

"Are you very unhappy here, then?" she wanted to know.

Kerry had to think for a minute, as if happiness had never entered into his considerations before. For all the fuss and bother, he was not unhappy here, no. He had to admit, in fact, that he'd never felt more alive, more purposeful, more in command of his own destiny before. He didn't have to admit that to Lucy, of course. Let her agonize a little after that fiasco with the fox.

"And where the deuce were you last night anyway?" he brusquely demanded. "If I'm stuck here for the nonce, I at least deserve some intelligent conversation."

"Oh, I was trying to answer your question about Aunt Clara's ghost. He's the second earl, poor man. You think you have problems! Why, he—"

The earl held up his hand. "No, don't tell me. I have more than enough difficulties laid in my dish without adding his. The rubies, the roof, Uncle Nigel—it's endless. If the second earl has been haunting the Abbey for the past century or so, I'm sure his situation is beyond my repair."

"I thought a Somerfield never backs down from a challenge."

"That's our motto, all right. A Somerfield never backs down, but he doesn't have to stand up either."

Chapter Eighteen

The direction of the vicar's sermon was that charity begins at home. The direction of the vicar's gaze seemed to indicate that charity ought to begin in the front pew.

And a dashed uncomfortable pew it was, too, Kerry thought, shifting his weight on the hard wooden bench next to his mother. Too bad the Brownes had refused to stay another day; perhaps they would have provided seat cushions in exchange for a few prayers of rejoicing in their son's recovery. Right now Kerry could use a pillow far more than another rug for the Grosvenor Square house.

And too bad the Brownes had refused his offer of that mongrel pup. Not in the City, they told him, with not too much regret. Even Diccon, the little traitor, thought Lucky would be happier in the country with his friend Hellraker. So now Kerry had the mixed breed trailing him and the stallion when they rode out. The earl swore Lucky's lolling tongue was a grin at his efforts to control the ill-humored horse.

The vicar was going on about feeding the hungry. Hades, Kerry thought, if the hefty cleric passed up second helpings, there'd be enough to feed half the village needy, whose eyes were also fixed on the front pew. Kerry couldn't help but be aware of the stares from the back rows of the little church, stares fastened on his superfine coat, biscuit pantaloons, and marcella waistcoat. Many of the parishioners were in ragged homespun, the women with threadbare shawls for warmth. Confound Demby! Kerry noted that neither Flint, the Prudlows, nor the Westcotts went to services here. They chose to attend the grander church in Farley, where their furs and furbelows would not make such a contrast. If Goldy Flint prayed here, he swore, they'd not be sitting on bare benches.

Then the earl's gaze drifted to the choir, where one voice was raised higher than all the others in joyful praise. Lucy was singing with the local members, standing out both in her brightly colored gown amid their white robes, and her slightly off-key rendition. The gown was almost a pinky-coral, far too dashing for church, but her hair was neatly coiled atop her head in a golden-copper halo of braids. And she looked happy as a grig.

That smile of hers shook his heart to its shaky foundations.

She was just a slip of a thing, Kerry reasoned, not a statuesque beauty like Miss Westcott; that was why he had an overwhelming desire to shelter her from sorrow, protect her from the world's evils, keep her smiling radiantly.

Dash it, he reminded himself, Lucy was not some vulnerable little schoolgirl. This she-devil could throw thunderbolts! She needed his looking after as much as he needed another indigent relative.

Still, when he shook the vicar's hand after the service, the earl found himself offering his work crew and some extra lumber to rebuild the church stairs. He also thought the abbey kitchens lost far too much to spoilage. Surely Cook could provide baskets of leftovers for the poor, rather than throw the foodstuffs away.

Of course that meant he'd have to find more slops for the hogs if table scraps were out, but Lucy's singing echoed in his ear the whole carriage ride home, sweet and only a little sour.

"Don't go getting in alt over this," he told her later, after spending all of that afternoon on what the vicar was pleased to call God's work, thus excusing the Sunday labor. Many of the locals, like Charlie the blacksmith and McGivven at the mercantile, had their own jobs to do on Monday, so they worked past dinner completing the stairs. They all supped on food the village women prepared from what Kerry had sent down from the Abbey. The dowager's dinner or not, it tasted better in the common room at Ned's pub.

"Why shouldn't I be pleased?" Lucinda insisted, wishing she could rub his sore shoulders as he groaned from the depths of a comfortable chair in the Abbey's library.

"Because it's not permanent, I told you. This doing good deeds and leading an exemplary life is not natural to me. Besides, it's all in my own self-interest anyway, don't you know."

She smiled. "Can't you confess you are doing something worthwhile just for its own sake?"

"What, like fixing the church steps so I don't break my neck next Sunday?" He put his feet up on a footstool and sighed.

"Like asking the vicar about starting a school."

"What's wrong with trying to lower my poor taxes by getting some of these people off the dole? I am a self-centered, arrogant, overdressed cod's-head, remember?"

"You forgot pigheaded. You are a good man, you just won't admit it. You wouldn't have been given this chance if there were no seed of decency to be nurtured. Know thyself, Kieren Somerfield."

"What about 'to thine own self be true'? I fear you're in for a big disappointment. What if at heart I really am a wastrel and a womanizer?"

"Then at least the church steps got fixed."

Not altogether discontent despite his warnings, Kerry settled back to enjoy a rest of the righteous weary, and the sight of Lucy worrying over her lists. She was tallying virtues versus vices, he supposed, the way Sidwell juggled assets and debits, but Sidwell never bit his tongue in concentration, at least not that Kerry ever noticed or cared. Nor did the earl believe he'd be satisfied to sit watching his secretary for any length of time. Lucy he could watch for hours, even if her hair was no longer trailing down her back in wanton disarray and her gown was no longer as diaphanous as an insect's wing. The grace of her movements, the rise and fall of her breaths, the softness of her cheek—

Well, he wasn't *terribly* discontented with the upright life. He had no urge to wager his watch on the roll of the dice or his last shillings on the speed of a raindrop, for instance. There was no burning ache for a cigarillo or a second, third, or fourth glass of brandy. And he didn't even want a woman, not too badly. Kerry laughed aloud at that thought, and the sound was so cheerful, Lucy laughed, too.

Tap-tap. The library door burst open before the earl could call "Enter." The dowager countess strode into the room, glaring into the shadowy corners. Aunt Clara hung back by the door, looking cautiously around.

"Just as I thought," the earl's mother declared, "there is no one in here with you." She crossed her arms across her chest. "I demand you stop this absurd habit at once."

Kerry had politely if stiffly risen at her entrance. "I always thought it a foolish practice myself, hopping up and down each time a lady stands. Won't you have a seat? You, too, Aunt Clara. Shall I ring for tea?"

Lady Stanford claimed the chair closest to the fireplace, where Lucy had been sitting. "Not that habit, you jackanapes. I mean this deplorable habit of speaking to yourself, as you well know. You already have the servants, what there are left of them, thinking you ready for a restraining device. You cannot wish the Westcotts to hear of this lunatic behavior. Bad enough they think you cannot sit a horse."

Aunt Clara arranged her black skirts and shawls onto the nearby sofa. "Were you speaking with Nigel, dear?" she wanted to know.

"No, it seems there is only one apparition allowed per customer. Have you ever actually seen Uncle Nigel, Aunt Clara?"

"Why, no, dear, I only hear his voice. Does your, ah, friend appear, in person, as it were?"

"Stop it, both of you!" The dowager shrieked, stamping her feet. "Clara might be the village eccentric, and my cross to bear, but I shall not have my son making such a cake of himself, do you hear me?"

"I am surprised Miss Westcott cannot hear you, Mother," Kerry said, getting up to close the door.

"Be sure she'll hear about this aberration of yours soon enough. Then you'll lose the gel for sure."

"Lose her? I hardly know her, Mother."

"What's that to the purpose? I never met your father until we joined hands at the altar."

No one commented on the success of that union. Aunt Clara leaned forward and asked, "But you do like Miss Westcott, don't you, dear?"

"She's a nice enough female, as far as debutantes go. I suppose I shan't mind dancing with her at that assembly tomorrow."

"You'd better do a dashed sight more than dance

with her, my boy," the dowager cautioned. "You'd better fix her interests all right and tight."

"Your mother is correct, dear. For once. Faint heart ne'er won fair lady, and all that."

"What, you, too, Aunt Clara? I said I'd dance with her. I cannot see rushing into anything more permanent for at least another meeting or two," he tried to joke. No one laughed.

Aunt Clara twisted a handkerchief in her hands. "I'm afraid there isn't time, dear. Rumor has it that Lord Westcott refuses to take Felicia back to London. Doesn't want to miss any more hunting, they say. Westcott's butler told Lady Prudlow's head groom that the marquis thinks another season would be a waste, since she turned down all the eligible partis, and that duke did not come up to scratch."

Lady Stanford took up the story: "So that twiddlepoop Westcott will be looking to get the gal fired off right here. If you don't snatch up the chit, he's liable to hitch Felicia to the first respectable beau, someone like Johnny Norris or something."

"So what? There will be other pretty girls, other heiresses."

"Oh, no, you wouldn't want to lose Miss Westcott, dear. So suitable. So dignified and polite. The way a countess should be."

Lady Stanford ignored the jibe. "You skip-brain, you don't have time to find another dowry. Bride, I mean. This is November. Have you forgotten that the next round of mortgage payments is due in January?"

Kerry had. He'd been thinking of what he could accomplish in the next week or so, for Lucy's sake, and in the long range, for income's sake. There was no way he could meet the payment due.

He almost missed his mother's next words: "My annuity is paid out in January, thank goodness, but you cannot expect help from me. I'll have to use my income to redeem my jewels, since you haven't seen fit to show your mother the respect due. So if you don't manage to snabble an heiress this month or next, we'll be living in your confounded pigpens, eating scraps."

"No, I am giving the table scraps to the poor." Kerry got up and started pacing.

"You gossoon, we *are* the poor!"

"I am impoverished, Mother; you do not need to be. You could be living in comfort in the Dower House if you hadn't squandered your annuity."

"You dare criticize me for a few paltry gambling debts? What happened to *your* income all these years?"

"Touché. Very well, I shall try to get to know your Miss Westcott at the assembly, to see if we suit. I am not making any promises, mind."

Aunt Clara came over to pat his hand before ringing for tea. "I'm sure you'll do everything proper, dear."

After Cobb wheeled in the tea cart and Lady Stanford poured, Kerry asked, "Will there be cards at this gathering, Mother?"

Lady Stanford looked as if she'd swallowed a lemon. "Why, do you hope to win a fortune instead of marrying one? That hasn't worked for you yet, Kieren."

"No, Mother, I shall be too busy doing my duty by the young ladies, inspecting their pedigrees, their bank balances, their teeth. Perhaps their hips for breeding."

Aunt Clara giggled into her cup. Lady Stanford returned hers to its saucer with a clatter.

"No," Kerry went on, "I was wondering about the cards for your sake, Mother, since the Stanford flaw seems to be transmitted through the marriage vows as well as through the blood." He swallowed the last of a cherry tart, his favorite, and carefully wiped his fingers on a serviette. "I shouldn't wish to see you sending us deeper into the River Tick while I am struggling to keep us afloat. If I so much as see you with a pasteboard in your hand, I'll tell Lady Westcott that your diamonds are fake."

Aunt Clara chimed in: "And I'll tell your beau Goldy that your bosoms are fake."

"Why, you jealous cat! Just because you never had a real man show any interest in you—"

"Real man, that shady character in corsets? How dare you compare that thatch-gallows to my sainted Nigel?"

"More tea, ladies?" Kerry asked before aspersions flew along with the Spode china. Aunt Clara held out her cup, but the dowager excused herself on account of the late hour.

"Some of us need our beauty sleep if we are to look our best for the assembly. Others wouldn't be helped by a week's rest."

After the door slammed shut, the earl turned to his aunt. "Aunt Clara, what if, hypothetically of course, Uncle Nigel turned out to be not such a paragon? If your hero had feet of clay? Would you still love him?"

"Oh, you are worried that you might discover later that Miss Westcott is pettish in the mornings or that she snores. Of course you would still love her, dear. I didn't know everything about dear Nigel before we were wed. It wouldn't have been at all the thing. But that's what love is, taking the bad with the good." Just when Kerry was about to breathe a sigh of relief, she added, "Naturally, however, I would never love a black-hearted rogue in the first place."

Naturally. "And, ah, you are certain it is Uncle Nigel chatting with you?"

"Quite certain, dear. Who else knows so much about the Abbey? I'm sure if it was your father, he'd be haunting *her*. Then again, he hardy spoke to her when he was alive, so why would he bother now?"

Chapter Nineteen

If anyone had suggested that Kieren Somerfield might someday stand ankle-deep in hog dung, directing inexperienced and incompetent footmen in corraling squealing porkers, Kerry would have laughed and said "When pigs fly."

He wasn't laughing, and they weren't flying. They'd come by slow, smelly, loud wagons, which he and Hellraker had to accompany, for Johnny Norris couldn't grab a piglet or hog-tie a sow.

Getting the stock distributed and settled took most of the morning. Catching escapees and repairing fences took most of the afternoon. Washing off the stench and the muck took two tubfuls of hot water.

At last Kerry felt clean enough to don the outfit Derek had selected from Demby's offerings for formal affairs. As opulent as possible without being ostentatious, the ensemble was more suited to a court presentation. The only thing missing was the ermine cape. Lord Stanford was complete to a shade in a velvet coat of charcoal gray, dove-gray satin knee breeches, sparkling white lace at the collar and cuffs of his shirt, with a waistcoat of burgundy brocade embroidered in silver thread. With his diamond stickpin in the cravat, he'd be bang up to the mark—if he could just tie the blasted neckcloth.

Fingers suddenly more used to handling shovels and saws instead of snuffboxes fumbled with yard after yard of discarded linen, to Derek's growing dismay. It was as if the earl's hands couldn't perform the functions logic demanded but emotion declined. He simply did not want to go to this ball. He did not want to pay court to the local toast.

Miss Westcott would be everything charming, he was sure, dressed to the nines, looking every inch the well-bred daughter of a well-breeched marquis. She would curtsy gracefully and smile demurely, expressing polite interest in whatever topic he chose to pursue. At least she did not chatter or giggle. If one could judge the daughter from the mother, the diamond would be content to stay in the shadows lording it over a small society but deferring in all things to her husband. Like Lady Westcott, Felicia was trained to be an accepting, complacent wife. Give her a full stable and a full closet, a few cicisbei to pay her flowery compliments, and Miss Westcott would be content to stay in Wiltshire while he pursued his own interests in London. Kerry could not begin to imagine Lucy tolerating such an arrangement.

He wondered how she danced. Lucy, not Miss Westcott. The heiress indubitably waltzed well, but not divinely. That would be Lucy's province. He recalled Lucy saying that she'd never been to a ball, but no matter. The way she glided around had to bespeak a grace unmatched by any London deb, no matter how practiced. Oh, how he wished he could be the one to lead her out for her first waltz.

Gads, he amended to himself, finally getting a perfect knot, how he'd like to hold her in his arms, period! "And that's not all I'd like to do," he said aloud, "so if you are reading my mind again, you may as well blush for something worthwhile."

"Oh, la," said Derek, fluttering his eyelashes.

The grandeur of the assembly rooms did not surprise Kerry, not with a pirate paying the shot. After Almack's austerity, this place seemed a veritable Xanadu, with flowers and festoons of ribbons.

The number and caliber of the guests was not surprising either. The well-dressed crowd being assisted from the expensive carriages and waiting on the receiving line could have passed for partygoers at Marlborough House. With little in the way of tonnish society unless one traveled to London, the landed and titled could not afford to be as high-nosed as the *belle monde* in town. A wealthy enough cit could buy his entree here, where he never could among the upper ten thousand.

The only surprise—nay, shock—at the evening's onset was the purple sash across Gideon Flint's ample chest. Atop the sash, which was atop a saffron coat, atop a puce waistcoat with cabbage roses imprinted on it, glittered a markedly recognizable bauble: the Order of the Knights of the Realm. The scapegrace smuggler had bought himself a knighthood! Speak of being more accepting of the lower ranks, everyone knew Prinny even-handedly distributed titles to anyone making a big enough contribution to the royal coffers.

So there the Earl of Stanford waited to shake the dastard's hand, his ancient title not keeping him from point-non-plus, and Gideon Flint, gold tooth flashing in his florid face, was a knight!

Things got worse. Word trickled through the receiving line that the prince had awarded Flint the knighthood for his service to the Crown, not just his pocketbook. The wine dealer's merchant ships—tidesmen, with no bark on them—had been carrying secret documents and couriers between France and Whitehall during the war. Gideon Flint was the espionage agent, and poor befuddled Uncle Nigel wallowed in France. That was beside the point, Kerry acknowledged to himself with no small amount of chagrin; Gideon Flint had done more for the war effort than the Somerfields ever had.

Unable to meet his mother's gloating smile, Kerry swallowed his humiliation and a mouthful of crow. He held out his hand and offered congratulations to Sir Gideon.

"Thankee, thankee, my lord. And that's Goldy to my friends. Sir Goldy. A word with you later, my boy, what?"

Goldy correctly opened the ball with the countess, the highest-ranking lady present. Kerry had the opening cotillion with Miss Westcott and asked her for the supper dance then also, as she was the wealthiest young lady present. The earl reasoned that Felicia's stately beauty saved him from being an arrant fortune hunter. He would have asked the prettiest girl at the assembly to dance even if she was the dustman's daughter, and he did appreciate her serene demeanor. What might be termed hauteur or arrogance or icy aloofness in Miss Westcott, he chose to call dignity. He would not pursue the prattling Prudlow pair if their grandmother left them each as rich as Croesus.

Which didn't mean he didn't dance with both the Prudlow girls, or perhaps the same one twice. His mother saw to that, in her self-conceived function as hostess for the ball, chivvying the bachelors out of their corners and onto the dance floor. The countess partnered the other Prudlow girl with Sidwell, who after meticulous research was deemed well enough connected, although through a cavalier branch, and whose wardrobe had to be augmented with Kerry's castoffs. Sidwell stammered, Priscilla—or was it Patricia? Both girls wore white—filled in the conversational gaps with double-time drivel, and they finished the contradanse well content with each other. The secretary had one of the heiresses on his arm for the supper dance. Kerry wished him well.

Johnny did his part, making sure Aunt Clara was settled amid her shawls and cronies, then staying on the sidelines to chat up the chaperones. He sent a footman for a cold glass of champagne for a flushed Miss Westcott after she returned from a particularly strenuous Scottish reel, then sat out the next dance with her while she recovered her breath. He even good-naturedly offered to try a one-handed waltz with her, which Kerry was pleased to see the beauty was not too proud to accept. That awkward set with Johnny improved Kerry's opinion of the incomparable far more than her graceful movements during the quadrille with him before supper ever could.

The earl purposefully seated Felicia at a small table, away from his family but unavoidably under the watchful eye of hers. He wanted to get to know her better. They spoke of the hunt and horses, mutual friends in London, the last plays they'd seen, and whether country life was preferable to city life. It was the same conversation Kerry'd had with innumerable females; he knew her no better after the raspberry ices than before the lobster patties.

Or perhaps he knew all there was to know? She liked parties but she loved to ride, preferred theater to opera, and did not, naturally, associate with the older, faster crowd he called friends.

No matter. He knew all he needed to know. She was beautiful, not a total widgeon, and rich. She wouldn't curdle his cream at the breakfast table, she wouldn't interfere with his pleasures, and she'd relieve his mind and pocketbook of a great many pressures. He asked for the next waltz, signifying his interest by requesting a third dance together; she accepted, indicating her receptivity to his suit. That was that.

As he rose to escort Miss Westcott back to the ballroom, Kerry felt a heavy hand on his shoulder.

"Care to step outside and blow a cloud, my lord?" Mr. Flint, Sir Goldy, asked, the countess at his side.

"No, thank you, sir. I am sorry, but I no longer smoke."

"Don't be a peagoose," Kerry's fond parent hissed in his ear. "Go on outside."

"I am promised to Miss Westcott for this coming set."

"Don't worry, I'll get young Norris to sit it out with her."

So instead of holding a warm and lovely perfumed woman in his arms, Kerry found himself out on the cold balcony, inhaling the noxious smoke from Goldy Flint's fat cigar. "I daresay the rubies could wait for a more comfortable setting," the earl commented, rubbing his hands together for warmth. "You must know I haven't the blunt for them anyway."

"Who's talking about the rubies?" Goldy asked as he spat out the end of his cigar. "I haven't called in the chits, have I? Mightn't be a gentleman in your sense of the word, but I've never dunned a lady yet." He took a long pull at the cigar and spat out more tobacco. "And I know you ain't got a feather to fly with; I had you investigated while I was in London."

"Why, of all the—"

"Wanted to know what kind of basket-scrambler you were before I took you on as stepson."

"—Presumpt—Stepson?"

"Aye. Didn't want any bailiffs at *my* door, or any jumped-up lordling bleeding me dry with begging his mama for handouts." Before Kerry could protest that outrageous affront, Flint was going on: "I saw as how you got yourself square with the duns, paid off your gambling debts, too, and haven't been back at the tables or the track since. And word is you are trying to make a go of the Abbey. I admire that in a man. Way I see it, you got off to a bad start. Bad influence and all." He held up a pudgy, be-ringed hand. "Don't mean to speak ill of the dead or any of that. And you're a man growed, not a boy, so it ain't for me to say how you should live your life. But you seem on the right track now, so I am prepared to make your fine mother an offer. With your permission, of course."

"I am, ah . . ." Kerry couldn't put a description to what he was feeling. Flabbergasted? Amused? Insulted? Flint could have knocked him over with a feather, Kerry was in such a swivet. The only other question he had was whether his stiff-rumped mother would accept this diamond in the rough, and on the fingers, pinned through the neckcloth, hanging from watchfobs, at that badge of honor. The rogue was a knight now! That wasn't quite an earl or a baron, but it was a start! And he could certainly keep the countess in the style to which she believed herself entitled.

"I wish you luck, Sir Goldy." Kerry hoped the other man never knew how much. "But you don't need my permission. The countess is her own woman. She will do what she wants." *She always has,* he almost warned.

"Still, I want this done all shipshape and Bristol fashion. Want your blessing on the match at least."

Kerry was able to assure Goldy of his approval. Anyone who'd take that expensive, querulous burden off his hands had the earl's wholehearted support. "And I'll be happy to put in a good word for you."

"Excellent, excellent. I'm prepared to come down heavy with the settlement, too, Stanford, so you don't have to worry about that."

A settlement? For bringing peace and prosperity to his household? "I don't expect any settlement, sir. Mother's annuity stops with her remarriage"—

and blessedly returns to the estate, but he didn't say that—"nor will she have a dowry, of course."

"I ain't asking for one, am I? The woman's prize enough in herself."

"I couldn't agree more. I just don't see that you should have to pay for the privilege, except for making provision in your will, of course, through the solicitors."

"I see what it is, your fine lordship. You're too proud to take Goldy Flint's money, no matter how much you need it."

"That's not it at all." That was it entirely.

Goldy tossed his cigar into the bushes. "Another noble fool gone hungry."

"I am not exactly hungry." And not quite a fool. "But there is one thing you could do for me . . ." He explained about Uncle Nigel.

Goldy slapped his fleshy thigh. "If that don't beat all. I'm surprised you toffs figured out how to put your pants on in the morning."

Kerry grinned. "That's why we have valets."

Goldy laughed and slapped his thigh again. "Well, consider it done. I have the prince's ear right now, and enough brass. I'll send a messenger to London tonight and another over to France. Have that blockhead back in no time to take that old crow Clara off your hands. Me and Margie off on our honeymoon, your decks'll be cleared for the new bride." He waved one hand in the vague direction of the ballroom. "Smart idea, that. Best you've had yet. Fine-looking woman."

"My mother?"

"Westcott's gal, lad. What are you waiting for?"

Kerry clenched his jaw. "I hardly know the lady."

"Cold feet, eh? Well, I'll get you the ruby engagement ring tomorrow. Make the diamonds your wedding present. I prefer to buy Margie her own jewelry anyway, something a little fancier."

The earl wondered what Goldy considered fancier

than diamonds, but he said, "About the jewels, why did you take them from the countess?"

"And let you think I was fleecing her? I know what you thought, Stanford, and I was sorry for it, but there was no other way. She was out of pin money and couldn't pay up. Terrible cardplayer is your mother, boy, but don't let on I said so. I liked the company and didn't want her to quit for lack of funds. It was either take the fripperies on tick or see her in the hands of the cent-per-centers. You wouldn't rather that, would you?"

Kerry held his hand out. "I owe you my thanks, and my apologies. I'll be proud to have you in the family."

"That's big of you, Stanford." Flint shook the earl's hand, almost squashing two fingers between his rings. "And don't worry about me embarrassing you in front of your fancy friends. Margie'll smooth out my rough edges before we come to stay at Grosvenor Square."

Chapter Twenty

"*I* have to go, you know."

"Yes, you asked Lord Westcott if you could call tomorrow. Today."

They were sitting in his bedroom in front of the fire, Kerry in the soft chair, Lucy on the fur rug not quite leaning against his knees. He could almost reach out and touch the coronet of curls atop her head, now mostly gold with just a tinge of chestnut. He didn't reach out, however, knowing the frustration of trying to capture a mirage. Instead, he tried to tell himself he was satisfied with her understanding, undemanding company.

It was late, or early. The ball had gone on long past the usual time for country gatherings, after Goldy's announcement of his betrothal to Lady Stanford. Kerry's permission must have been taken for granted, because there was no more than a moment's pause between their return to the ballroom and the new knight's public proclamation. Footmen were already pouring fresh champagne before the earl kissed his mother's proffered cheek.

The neighbors did not appear perturbed by the

alliance. Lord Stanford, in fact, was the only one the least surprised by the engagement, everyone else having long been aware which way the wind blew. Even Aunt Clara was *aux anges*, now that Flint was a knight, and promising to take her nemesis on a long bridal journey. She couldn't wait to get home to tell Nigel they'd have the place almost to themselves, but was content to bide at the assembly until nearly dawn, savoring the betrothal as her own emancipation.

The local gentry were not reticent about expressing their approval to Lord Stanford. Goldy was a favorite, it seemed. And his champagne was excellent.

Now there were only a few hours left before Kerry's appointment with Lord Westcott.

"I have to do it, Lucy," he said.

"I know."

"Even with the rubies back, Uncle Nigel's pardon assured, and my own gambling debts paid, hard work just isn't enough. I have to do it," he said again, as if the repetition would make the deed more palatable.

Lucy nodded. "All those people are depending on you for their living."

"And all those lady pigs are depending on me to find them a boar."

"And this wonderful old house is falling apart."

"And the stables are empty, the fields are a disgrace, the cottages are hovels. And you."

"Me?" Lucy looked up so he could see that her eyes were a warm hazel now, not that startling green of when he first encountered her.

"You, Miss Faire. Have you noticed your appearance lately? Your gown is pink. Not rose, not coral, but pink, and with a white gauze overskirt that would be acceptable at Almack's. You appear to have all your unmentionables in place, even gloves, and there's not a trace of paint anywhere. You've even begun to smell like flowers. Lilies-of-the-valley, I think. Can't you see, the odds must have turned to our favor. We're almost there. We cannot quit now."

Lucinda savored the "we" and smiled her most winning smile, dimples and all.

Kerry groaned. "Oh, Lord, I don't want to go out to Westcott's."

Lucy's smile dimmed, but she told him: "Felicia is a lovely girl. Refined, well-educated. She'll make you a good wife."

"An accepting, polite wife. Is that what I want, someone who will accept me for what I have—the title, the Abbey—instead of who I am? Oh, we'll have a marriage like every other in the ton, doing the season with our separate friends, meeting at various dinners and dances. Ever so proper. Then she'll be increasing and staying on in the country, and I'll pursue my own pleasures in town."

"You don't have to return to your former devil-may-care ways, you know."

"Ah, but I will. Marriage to Miss Felicia Westcott will not change the tiger's stripes. I would not have minded so much once." Before I met you, he thought, but did not say. "But now? How can I repeat the marriage vows, knowing I intend to break them? Knowing my wife is likely thinking the same, that as soon as she presents me with an heir she can have her discreet little *affaires*?" He found distraction in winding his watch, but then he listened to its working, and heard his freedom ticking away. "Oh, how I wish things could be different."

"And I," Lucy said softly, aching for what could never be.

Kerry shook himself. "But they aren't. I was born an earl with an earl's duties and responsibilities, even if I am somewhat tardy in coming to them and needed a nudge from the netherworld to accept them. Right?"

She tried for a smile. "Right."

"At least I don't have to go to Westcott with

mounds of debts and Uncle Nigel hanging over my head. And here I thought hell would freeze over before I was grateful to Gideon Flint. But you're not wearing ice skates, are you?" he teased, looking down to where dainty pink satin slippers hid under her skirts. Pink satin *dancing* slippers. "I thought you'd come to the ball, since you'd never been."

"Oh, I was talking to the second earl. He says—"

"Not now, Lucy, please. Westcott is all the duty I can handle in one day." She started to interrupt, but he held up a hand. "No. Right now there is only one thing I want to hear, the strains of a waltz. Do you think it possible for us to have a dance, just this once? Johnny did it with one hand; we ought to be able to manage something, don't you think?"

The earl hummed a popular dance tune and explained the steps. Lucy stepped into his arms, or thereabouts, and hummed along. Yes, lilies-of-the-valley, and yes, the tingly glow he remembered, that warmth, and almost electric shock of desire. And yes, she hummed slightly out of tune. "Do you play the pianoforte like every other well-bred young female?" he asked when he could, hoping she did not hear the quaver in his voice.

"No, my father thought that led to familiarity. You know, young people standing around singing together. I play the harp."

"Gabriel is going to love you, angel." Kerry laughed and twirled her around.

Derek tiptoed into his master's chamber, saw the earl dancing with an invisible partner, and quickly backed out, tears in his eyes.

The rubies arrived early the next morning, along with an emerald ring for the countess. The emerald was as big as a bird's egg and the surrounding diamonds made the Crown Jewels look tawdry.

"And that's nothing," an exuberant Goldy informed them all over breakfast. "The necklace that goes with the ring is so wide, you won't even see Margie's chest under it."

Before Aunt Clara could ruin the old man's breakfast with a remark about the dowager's chest, Kerry thought to start preparing her for Uncle Nigel's return.

"Oh, no, dear, once a person is dead, they stay dead. You must be a little more disturbed than I thought. I mean, ghosts are all well and good, but just think what would happen if your father should decide to return now?" Which ruined everyone's breakfast anyway.

Ruby ring in hand, or pocket, as it were, Kerry set out on a raw, dreary day that matched his mood. Even the angels are weeping, he thought as a cold rain started to fall, but he couldn't see Lucy upstairs in his bed, crying her eyes out.

Rain dripping off the rim of his beaver hat and down his collar, Kerry handed Hellraker's reins to a sturdy-enough-looking groom and started to walk up the steps of Westcott Hall. Now he knew how a condemned man must feel on his way to the gallows. Every step was an eternity, and over all too soon.

A footman showed the earl to the gun room, where Lord Westcott was cleaning a hunting rifle. Marvelous, thought Kerry, looking at the stuffed trophies on the wall, the man was preparing to add an earl to his collection.

"Sit, Stanford, sit," the marquis invited him. "You look like your knees are giving out. Haven't tamed that brute of a horse yet, eh?"

"No, Hellraker and I have come to terms. He hasn't tried to take a piece out of my flesh in days now. I doubt he'll ever be a trustworthy mount, but he'll never be a dull ride either."

Westcott put down his rag and ramrod. "Must be another cause has you green about the gills, then, what?" He laughed, but sobered quickly. "Shouldn't tease about a serious matter. Why, I remember when I had to ask my lady's father's permission. Worst day of my life. Couldn't even decide if I wanted him to say yea or nay."

"Then you do know why I am come?"

"I daresay the whole shire knows why you are come. Can't keep such a thing quiet in the country. Young hellion with debts, mortgages, expensive tastes"—he gave a sharp, assessing look at Kerry's corbeau-colored coat and fawn breeches—"comes asking to speak to an heiress's papa, what do you think?" He sighted down the rifle's barrel.

"I think you insult Miss Westcott, begging your pardon, my lord," Kerry said quickly. "The lady is beautiful, intelligent, and talented, from what I heard of her pianoforte playing. I think any man, no matter his circumstances, would be tempted to offer for your daughter."

"Well spoken, Stanford, well spoken." The marquis put the rifle down and stared at the earl. "But you ain't what I had in mind for a son-in-law."

"I understand completely, my lord, and I am sure I would feel the same way if I had a daughter." Kerry stood to leave.

"Hold on. You didn't let me finish. I was looking higher, not that an earldom is anything to sneeze at, but you said yourself the gel is an incomparable, and my fortune has nowhere to go but to her and her get. But that didn't work out."

Not for the first time, Kerry wondered why the hoped-for duke had cried off before a formal announcement. He did not think it would be politic to ask right now. He cleared his throat instead.

Lord Westcott picked up another rag and some oil. While he caressed the rifle's wooden stock, he went on: "I ain't saying you're not an out and outer, for I made a parcel on you and those bays, but there's no denying you ain't at first oars these days. Penniless knight of the baize table ain't what I wanted for my little girl either."

Kerry started to rise again.

The rifle was aimed at his head. He sat down, wishing the man would just put him out of his misery already, like the other stuffed victims around the room.

"Nor a rakehell, a town beau, or one of those man-milliners neither." He glared again at the shoulder-hugging cut of the earl's jacket. The glass-eyed squirrel on the table next to Kerry seemed friendly by comparison.

"I'm sorry to have taken your time, my lord. I'll just be—"

"But my girl is fussy, and my wife has a yearning to have her close by. Only chick, don't you know. So I gave you a second look. And I liked what I saw. Oh, not at the hunt, but a better-trained animal will show you to advantage next time, I'm sure. No, I mean how you're trying to make something of that ramshackle property you inherited. I said to myself, here looks like a fellow who's tired of sowing his wild oats. Maybe he's ready to settle down now."

"Yes, sir, I believe I am. And I also believe that I can make your daughter a good husband."

Westcott nodded. "A good woman always has a steadying influence, and they say there's no better husband than a reformed rake." He picked up the rifle again. "I'd hate to find out otherwise."

"No, sir, never." And there Kerry'd been worried about forswearing his vows before the Church. Hell, the Church didn't shoot something before breakfast every day. Kerry stopped wondering why the duke had backed off. "Then I take it I have your permission to pay my addresses to Miss Felicia?"

"Her answer is yes, we already discussed it. Our solicitors can settle the rest of the details. Felicia's dowry is substantial, but most of the real money will come when I'm gone. You'll understand, I'm sure, if I insist the bulk of that gets tied up for my grandchildren."

Kerry understood the marquis didn't trust him out of his rifle range. Of all the humiliating, aggravating—no matter, the dowry was enough. He nodded. "Thank you, my lord, for giving me this chance. If I might see Miss Felicia now?"

"I told you, you can arrange for the calling of the banns. Daresay you'll want the wedding as soon as can be."

"Whatever Miss Westcott desires. However, I hope to hear the acceptance to my proposal from her own lips before there is any formal announcement." He wanted to make deuced certain the girl wasn't being coerced into anything, after knowing of Lucy's plight.

Lord Westcott started polishing the rifle butt again, not meeting the earl's eyes. "Well, she ain't here right now. Your man Norris came by earlier on his way to the Widow Welford's place, looking to get the address of that breeder Tige bought his prize boar off of. I told young Norris the boar was the meanest bastard there ever was, but he wanted to check before the widow moved away."

"Yes, Johnny told me he meant to come this way. And Miss Felicia?"

"She was going out for her ride, so went along with him. Nothing wrong in that," the marquis hastened to add. "They've been friends since leading strings, and her groom went, too. Nothing to concern yourself about."

The earl studied the stuffed squirrel. "Of course not."

"Young Norris is a good man," Westcott said in reassurance, although whom he was reassuring was questionable.

"The best," Kerry agreed. "I trust him implicitly. In fact, I don't know how I could get on without him. He's used to commanding from his days in the army, and the men respect him more than they respect me. I still haven't earned their esteem, even after breaking my back alongside them. And Johnny's truly knowledgeable about farming, a wizard at the latest methods after studying all the journals and articles. Most admirable of all to my thinking, he's managed to keep his good humor and open manner despite all the troubles he's seen. A lesser man would have turned bitter under his handicap. Meeting John Norris again was one of the luckiest days of my life, along with the day I met your daughter, of course."

"You make me wish I'd hired him on myself. I always thought a man should manage his own estates. Not get robbed blind that way. But now I'm not so sure. I'm getting too old, my days are too few to waste on all that busy work."

The earl stood to go. "I wish you the best, but I shan't part with Johnny, not even in exchange for your daughter's hand. Good try though, my lord." They shook hands amiably and parted after the earl said, "Please give my respects to Miss Felicia, and tell her that I shall call tomorrow. And better hunting next time."

Chapter Twenty-one

*T*omorrow was too busy, so the earl had Johnny bring Miss Westcott some straggling flowers from the rundown conservatory, on his way to meet a delivery of equipment.

The earl, meanwhile, was rebuilding cottages. According to Sidwell, the outlay in materials, with the workmen already on payroll, would be repaid quickly in increased rent revenues and decreased labor costs. Lord Stanford could take a short-term loan, with the pigs as collateral, for whatever was needed to make the abandoned places habitable.

Increasing his indebtedness did not sound wise to Kerry, but Sidwell was persuasive, and so was Lucy, reminding him of those poor families he'd seen at church, some even his own ex-tenants, who would leap at the chance for a workable, livable farmstead. So Kerry and his squad of footmen turned into shinglers and thatchers, whitewashers, and hammer-wielders. Then there were applications at the bank, interviews with prospective tenants, and endless, useless explanations to Goldy Flint why he wouldn't borrow money from his future stepfather or father-in-law. And there were those few hours, late at night, when he sat with Lucy by the fire, talking of the day's accomplishments, his plans for the morrow. With every family he moved in, every roof he made sound, she took on a new radiance. Her gown was the pink of wildflowers, with long sleeves and a neckline almost to her collarbone, with lace and flowing ribbons. She wore a wreath of twined violets in her strawberry-blond hair.

The earl sent Johnny back to Miss Westcott's, begging her apology and making his excuses. "You go, John, you've known her longer; you'll know what to say that won't appear an insult. A note seems cold, and Sidwell would only stutter. Tell her I'll be there tomorrow for sure."

But tomorrow Uncle Nigel came home.

"Never let it be said that Goldy Flint ever does things by half, my lad, no siree."

Lord Stanford wouldn't be saying it, no siree. Not only had the wine merchant fetched Nigel Somerfield home almost overnight, bag and baggage, dressed like a gentleman, but he'd also fetched Nigel's entire French family, in-laws, children, grandchildren. Not only had Goldy seen to Nigel's pardon, he'd also had him made a knight while he was at it.

"Seemed the best to do, quiet down some of the talk, don't you know."

Kerry didn't know how anyone thought to keep an invasion of the Wiltshire countryside by a ménage of French fishermen quiet, but he nodded, inquiring only how Goldy accomplished such a thing.

"That was the easy part. I just said he was my contact on French soil, passing messages to my men about troop strength, planned movements, all that flummery. Said he'd gotten there by accident, which Lud knows was no more than the truth, and stayed on out of service to the country."

"Which country?" Kerry couldn't help asking, watching as the third small child was handed out of the traveling carriage.

"Don't look so worried, nevvy," Uncle Nigel said as he sadly watched Aunt Clara being carried back to the sofa after her third swoon. "I don't mean to stay on and be an embarrassment to anyone. I know there's no way English society can accept this." He waved his hands in a Gallic gesture, encompassing the chattering children and somber adults who were huddled together at the other end of the drawing room, away from the odor of burning feathers.

"I appreciate all you've done, more than I can ever say. You, Kerry, and my new brother-in-law. Oh, I know Goldy ain't any kind of relation to me at all, but he's done more than my own brother ever did. Your father could have searched a little harder, I always felt, Kerry. And I tried to get messages to him. Don't know if any got through, but he never sent any back." Nigel wiped a tear from his eye with a large red handkerchief.

"I never knew, Uncle Nigel, or I would have tried to help."

"I know you would, lad. You were always a good boy. But what could you have done, a little nipper? Besides, that's all water under the bridge. You got Goldy here to lend a hand, and that's all that matters. He's giving us, all of us, passage on one of his ships bound for the West Indies so I can see about that copper mine now that the revolutions there are over. Should be worth a fortune by now. If not, we aim to set up a fishing cartel, Goldy and me. I hear they've got big fish there in the warm waters. Salt 'em and ship 'em, I say."

"But you'll stay awhile? After all these years . . ."

They both looked to where the countess and Goldy were helping Clara back to her feet.

"No, no amount of explaining will make what I did come right, not even with a *sir* before my name.

Clara never cared for things like that, no more than I did. I just wanted to come by to thank you, and to see ... once more ... and to beg forgiveness." Tears were streaming down Nigel's weathered face. Kerry had to turn away lest his own watery eyes betray him. "I'll ... I'll be getting out of your life again."

Aunt Clara had tottered over on Goldy's arm. She reached out a trembling hand and touched Nigel's cheek, brushing away a tear. "But you've never been out of my life, dearest."

Kerry and his mother shepherded everyone out of the room so the reunited pair could have some privacy. The dowager and Goldy led the adults away to the dining room for a hastily prepared luncheon, and the earl gathered his small charges for a foray on the kitchens. These new cousins of his spoke a French like nothing his tutors ever taught, but porridge was a universal language, and so were piglets and a puppy afterward.

Aunt Clara decided to travel with Nigel. She couldn't remember a word of her schoolgirl French beyond *j't'aime*, but that was enough. She adored her new children, was eager for a new adventure, and vowed never to let Nigel out of her sight again, even if she had to take up rod and reel.

She would miss Kerry, of course, and the Abbey where she'd spent the last twenty years, and that kind gentleman who kept her company so many lonely nights. Waving her handkerchief out of the coach window, she made Kerry repeat his vow to offer comfort to the poor fellow.

"Yes, Aunt Clara," he called back, "as soon as I take care of some pressing personal matters myself."

He rode straight off to Westcott Hall, Lucky frisking and barking at Hellraker's heels again now that the children were gone. Kerry kept yelling at the foolish mutt to shut up, the noise was giving him a headache.

Miss Westcott was shopping in Farley. Did he want to wait? No, the earl had too many other matters to attend to, and once a woman started shopping, who knew how long she'd be? He'd call again the next day.

And he whistled all the way home. What headache?

Lord Stanford's headache returned that afternoon when his mother announced they were expected at Lady Prudlow's for a dinner honoring her and Sir Goldy's betrothal. Kieren could not dare refuse, she declared, lest people think he disapproved of her engagement. Besides, the Westcotts would be there, and what in the world was he thinking of, making that poor girl the butt of wagers and cruel jests?

All the neighbors were there at the dinner, along with the vicar, some tonnish houseguests of the younger Prudlows', a few sporting gentlemen up for Westcott's hunt, and a gaggle of ladies of a certain age come to bear old Lady Prudlow company in the country fastness.

They were all waiting, wondering when the rake would retire from the bachelor lists, watching to see when he'd ask Felicia to stroll through the portrait gallery or amble among the potted palms in the conservatory. Tarnation! Kerry felt he was back in the gun room with all those dead creatures staring at him through glassy eyes. Hang it, he was not going to conduct his engagement like a side show at the local fair. Besides, he'd forgotten to bring the deuced ring.

So Kerry stayed on with Ralph Norris long after the gentlemen rejoined the ladies after port, continuing their discussion of winter wheat. Felicia was already at the pianoforte, Johnny turning pages, while the Prudlow girls sang. So the earl chatted with Major Lawrence about the local terrain, with the dowager Duchess of Farnham about her rheumatics, and with the vicar about cushions for the church pews. He even took his turn singing with the others, but he did not take Felicia on a turn about the room.

"I have an appointment to call on her tomorrow, Mother," he said, resting his aching head back on the squabs during the carriage ride home. The countess did not make too many disparaging remarks about his mental capacity or his manhood, just enough that he proposed she and Goldy move up the date for their own wedding.

At home, the earl found that he could not sleep. Lucy hadn't come, so he decided to go exploring and satisfy his vow to Aunt Clara. He wrapped his dressing gown more securely around him, put an extra candle in his pocket, and set out for the east wing and the second earl.

He didn't see the haunt, but he did see stars shining through the ceilings, bird droppings on some of the warped floors, and at least one bat. Devil a bit, this was more than he and a handful of amateur handymen could fix. Such a mess needed architects, engineers, skilled carpenters, and plasterers. Since he didn't require the rooms, especially with Aunt Clara and his mother moving out, and couldn't afford their upkeep, it might be better to tear the east wing down. Then again, the whole blasted thing might fall down of its own accord before he had the wherewithal to make repairs.

Kerry hefted a fireplace poker over his head to check one ceiling for dry rot. It was there, all right, enough so his slight disturbance brought half the plasterwork down on his head.

Now he had a headache for sure. As he lay on the ground, waiting for the dust to clear and the room to stop spinning, he thought he saw a gentleman in doublet and hose step out of the wainscoting. He shook his head, which was a definite mistake, for a black curtain came down over his eyes.

"Thou hast done well, lady. I never bethought myself the varlet could be brought to duty and honor."

"Oh, he only needed a nudge, my lord," Lucy answered. "He's a fine man, truly."

"I doth not contradict a lady. 'Struth, shalt indeed be an heir soon?"

"The good Lord willing. I am sure Lord Kieren is."

"Hmm. He looks a bonny lad, not unlike mine own self in bygone days. Why is he garbed like the veriest hired mourner, forsooth, in those somber hues? Lady Clara had reason and respect for her widow's weeds. What hath this scoundrel?"

"Your many-times-great-grandson is considered a nonpareil, Lord Stanford. Those dark colors are the height of fashion."

"Fie on fashion! The knave depresseth mine eyes. And thou, my lady, with thy gown buttoned chin to toe, might be in a nunnery. Bah! Hast thou told him about me?"

"No, my lord. I tried, but he has been too concerned with other matters."

"He be as thick-headed as ever, but thou art too much the Lady Fair to speak it."

Lucy chuckled. "I believe it would take a miracle to change his stubbornness, not just a tiny push."

"A kick in the noble posterior might do it. Too bad the jobberknoll doth not know what a treasure he possesseth."

Kerry tried to raise his head to say that he did know. He knew without a doubt that Lucy was the best thing that ever happened to him. And he tried to ask the old gentleman if there was aught he could do about it, but his tongue wouldn't find the words and the mist wouldn't clear from his brain.

Chapter Twenty-two

"*If* you had to choose between love and duty, my lord, which would you select?"

"What is this, Lucy, an oral examination to pass through the Pearly Gates?"

A cold rain falling through the new hole in the east wing's ceiling had woken Kerry. He'd stumbled down the hall, covered in plaster dust, moaning. Cobb the butler lost two years from his life. This morning the earl had awakened much too early when his valet entered to find piles of reddened towels and blood on his sleeping—or murdered—master's head. Derek's shrill cries had the earl off his mattress and lunging for a weapon to defend the household against marauding Huns. Naked.

Derek ran off, his hand over his mouth, before he disgraced himself further. So now Kerry was trying to dress himself for his morning call. Rain was still falling in torrents, his hair would never cover the gash on his forehead, and Miss Westcott was waiting. Kerry was not in the mood for metaphysical word games.

Lucy tried again, although she was distracted by

watching him shave, the way he lifted his chin and turned to the mirror, just so. "Um, well, if two people loved each other very much but you had the power to come between them, and felt it was your duty to do so, would you weigh their happiness against your honor?"

"Cut line, Lucy. All this roundaboutation isn't like you. How can I answer when I don't know the circumstances? Like if I saw a couple eloping, would I cry rope on them? Why should I if they don't mind facing the scandal?"

"But if one of the elopers were your own fiancée?"

He put down the razor and turned to her, his face half covered in lather. "Just what are you saying?"

Lucy studied the buttons at her wrists. "Felicia and Johnny Norris. They love each other and have since they were children playing together."

"And they are eloping?"

"Oh, no, they would never do what I did. Miss Westcott is too aware of the impropriety and Johnny has too much honor to bring her such disgrace."

"But he doesn't have enough honor to offer in form?" Kerry asked angrily.

Lucy shrugged. "He knew he would have been refused. Besides, he cannot provide for her. No man of integrity would offer love in a cottage to the woman he adored."

"Instead, he'll make me a cuckold, is that it?"

"How could you even think that of John Norris? He's your friend! And much too honorable to even consider such a thing as making love to another man's wife, or wife-to-be."

"You're right. I was judging him by myself. Johnny Norris is too fine a man. But what about Felicia?"

"She loves him, but she knows her duty, too. A wealthy marquis's daughter does not marry a land steward or a half-pay officer."

"Instead, she'd marry a half-mad earl and we'll all be miserable," he said in bitter tones.

"No, you are all reasonable adults. You will all try to make the best of things. Felicia would never show her unhappiness; Johnny would never wear his heart on his sleeve; and you would never have known if I hadn't told you."

"Then why did you, dash it? I thought you wanted me to marry a fortune, settle down, try to be generally faithful, beget my heirs."

"I did. I do. But I want your happiness also. I thought you could find it with Miss Westcott. I was wrong, for you cannot be happy considering your own well-being ahead of their chance for love."

"Not even for the Westcott fortune? You had me damned near convinced I could." He furiously wiped his face with a towel, spattering lather at the mirror. "And what about you if I do not fulfill my obligations, marry well, and secure the succession? What happens to your chances if I am not a reformed character?"

Lucy twisted the ribbons of her gown between her hands. "I don't know, but I am willing to take the chance." His happiness was worth any sacrifice to her.

"Well, I am not, damn it! We can all be comfortable, you said it yourself. And there's no guaranteeing that if I don't drop the hanky Johnny will, or will be accepted, so that's a bad gamble against your odds of success. If I gave up Miss Westcott, I'd really only be giving up the money. Even I know money isn't everything; just look at the fortunes that have drifted through my hands these past days. But you, you are talking about eternity!"

"If the money is the only reason for offering, you should never do it! Give her up, Kerry," she begged.

"I told you I was wrong. Happiness does not have to be forfeited for duty, and I do not mean just Felicia and Johnny's happiness. You deserve the opportunity to find your own true love someday, too."

Someday seldom came twice. A hard knot formed in Kerry's chest, squeezing down. If he couldn't marry where he wished, what matter whom he wed? What did any of it matter?

"I'll think about it," he told her, turning back to complete his shave. The water was as cold as the chill in his heart.

He should have taken the closed coach in this confounded never-ending rain, but the horses were ancient and the dowager's driver was older than that. In London the earl would not have given a second thought for the hackney driver he'd have hired, sitting out in the teeming downpour. Here, people's feelings had to be considered, their welfare taken into account. Now he was having to be responsible for their blasted happiness!

Felicia and her mother were waiting for him in the parlor, embroidery in their laps. He admired the fancy work, commented on the wretched weather, and gratefully accepted a glass of sherry after his cold, wet ride. A polite interval later, Lady Westcott recalled a message for her housekeeper and excused herself.

How civilized, Kerry thought: the heiress trigged out in style, the chaperone conveniently gone missing, the father likely down the hall cleaning a pistol. He took a deep breath.

"Miss Westcott, do you know why I have asked for an interview this morning?"

"Yes, my lord, I think I do." She seemed uncertain whether to continue with her embroidery or to stuff it away somewhere. Kerry ended her confusion as to the proper mien for entertaining a proposal by lifting the cloth out of her hands and sitting beside her on the couch. He wanted to see her face.

"And do you wish to marry me, Miss Westcott?"

"I am deeply cognizant of the great honor you do

me, my lord," she recited, having that part down pat.

"But that is not what I asked, Miss—blast it, Felicia. I am asking if you would rather I didn't ask, if you would rather marry someone else."

She stared at her hands, the correct, reserved beauty not having a suitable response to such an inquiry. "My lord?"

"Fiend seize it, do you love Johnny Norris?"

Felicia grabbed back her embroidery and started setting fast, furious stitches. "My lord Stanford, you offered for me, and my papa said he accepted for me. That is all that need concern you."

"As I told your father, I prefer to do my own asking. And I do believe it concerns me that my intended might be wishing me to Jericho. Call it vanity if you will—I know that's a great sin of mine; I am working to improve—but my pride does not gracefully accept being a female's second choice."

"Mr. Norris has never sought my hand. We are friends, that's all."

"But do you love him?" he persisted, tipping her chin up so she was forced to meet his penetrating gaze. "Please, I must know the truth. Now is not the time for those social lies, for saying what you think I wish to hear, or what is correct for the situation. I swear no one shall ever know what we discussed here. Do you love Johnny Norris?"

She whispered it. "Yes."

"And would you accept him if he did ask for your hand in marriage? Please be honest, my dear, all our lives depend on it."

"He refuses to ask," she snapped. "He thinks of himself as less of a man, now that he's lost his arm. He cannot ride to the hunt, and swears that was all that commended himself to me in the first place, the gudgeon, since he has neither title nor money. As if I didn't have enough money for both of us, or cared only about foolish titles. He says he is not good enough for me."

"When we both know he's one of the finest, bravest men anywhere."

"He will not listen." She dabbed her eyes with a scrap of lace.

Kerry patted her hand. "It's hard for a man to swallow his pride. We seem to have such a surfeit of it."

"Well, it is hard for a female to wait, dwindling into an old maid, seeing all your friends marry and start their nurseries, listening to your parents despair."

"It would be worse to marry without affection, to live your whole life without love. And you cannot have thought of your pain living so close to him. He'll eventually marry, have children of his own. You'd see him at church, at parties, and you'd always wonder what might have been."

She was biting her lip to keep from crying. Kerry handed her his own handkerchief, more practicable for such a damp day. "I'd hate like hell having my wife wishing I were another man."

"I wouldn't—"

"If you loved him, you couldn't help yourself."

The earl got up and poured a glass of wine for Felicia and another for himself.

She started: "But my father . . ."

"I'll say we decided we wouldn't suit."

"No, he'll never allow that. If you ask, I have to accept."

"I haven't asked, have I? What could be easier? I'll tell him I changed my mind, that I decided I really don't wish for leg shackles at this time. So wearying in the country, don't you know," he drawled in a dandy's affected tones, "away from the tables and the ladies."

Felicia encouraged him with a watery smile, so he went on: "Why, when I'm finished, he'll be thrilled to welcome a steady character like our

Johnny. No reckless past, no unsavory habits, no worries of him gambling away your inheritance. I'll even throw in a hint or two about Uncle Nigel returning to live with me."

"And all those children?"

"Marvelous, ain't it, what a little scandal can do? Your father will be relieved to see a real hero ride up to your door. Besides, he's no fool. Getting such a dab hand as steward for free is no mean feat."

"But will he get him? I mean, this is all very pleasant speculation, but what happens when Johnny does not propose?"

"Oh, he will. First I'll dismiss him. That should send him either here or back to the gin bottle. If he thinks to head for the decanter, I'll tell him you are pining away for him, in a veritable decline. If he still doesn't make the push, I'll break his arm."

"My lord! He has only one arm!"

"So it will be an easier task than I thought. I'll guarantee he shows his handsome phiz at your door, and leave the rest to you. A slightly compromising situation . . . ?" At her gasp he said, "No, I didn't think so. No matter, those tear-filled blue eyes ought to wring his heart, and that trembling lip you showed me a moment ago. And if you'll just swear you won't accept anybody else, but will wither away like the last leaf of autumn, he'll come 'round." He smiled at her, teasing, but then grew serious again. "Uh, there isn't another nobleman waiting in the wings somewhere by any chance, trading taxidermy tips with the marquis or anything? Viscount? Baron? Lowly baronet?"

"No, you were Papa's last hope for a title, my lord."

"Thank goodness, or I'd have to break their arms, too."

Felicia's lips twitched, her polite mask restored. "But what about you, my lord? You are showing gallant selflessness, but you did ask Papa for permission to pay your addresses. Shall you be very disappointed?"

"Shall I mind being the spurned lover?" Kerry brushed a speck of lint off his sleeve. "Shall I drown my sorrows in the fleshpots of London, preying on your conscience? I understand that half the gentlemen in town have thrown themselves at your feet, so naturally you might worry about my wounded sensibilities. Do not, for I have none. I beg your pardon for being blunt, ma'am, but my heart was not involved, no more than yours. And do not attribute any great nobility to me, my dear, for the sacrifice, though great in light of your abundant charms, is mostly mercenary. That, I am assured you will agree, is an unworthy sentiment."

"I don't care what you say, Lord Stanford, I think you have been wondrously noble, a true friend to Johnny and myself. And you must have tender sensibilities whether you admit them or not, else you'd never understand our plight. You'd never place our happiness over your material considerations. Few men would. I think your heart *is* involved, just elsewhere."

The earl's silent study of the tassel on his Hessian boot was confirmation enough.

"You must love her very much."

"Yes, I'm afraid I do."

"But you do not offer for her?"

Kerry just shook his head.

"Then I hope everything comes right for you and your lady whatever the impediments, the way you have made things possible for Johnny and me."

"No, it can never be made right. She is ... You might say she is from a different world."

Chapter Twenty-three

$\mathscr{K}$erry and the stallion slogged back home through the continuing downpour. Instead of heading straight for the stables and a hot bath, the earl directed Hellraker toward the south edge of the property, where Johnny and the men were working on the drainage ditch despite the rain.

"Pack it in," Kerry yelled over the raging storm. "The men are all soaked through, and none of you will be any good to me if you all come down with inflammation of the lungs. Besides, this land has been flooded since Englishmen were painting themselves blue. One more storm won't make a ha'penny's difference."

The workers cheered considerably when he told them to go on home, change into dry clothes, and have an afternoon holiday at his expense. He poured a handful of coins into work-roughened hands. "Go warm yourself with Ned's mulled ale at the pub if you wish. Just be ready to work even harder tomorrow."

Johnny took a little more convincing to aim in the right direction.

"Don't let your foolish pride stand in the way, man," Kerry shouted to be heard. "Pride won't keep you warm at nights, or sit by your fireside, or give you children."

"But you want her!" Johnny protested.

"No, I only wanted a rich, well-bred, well-behaved, and beautiful bride. Felicia happened to fill the bill. That doesn't mean I want her, or need her. Not like you, who need her to be your other half. And she needs you, too. She loves you, man!"

Johnny kept arguing about misalliances and unequal matches until Kerry almost did plant him a facer. "It's pouring rain, damn you, and I swear mildew is forming inside my boots! Will you listen to yourself going on how you love her too much to ruin her life? Would you be happy with another woman?"

"No, of course not," Johnny swore, hunched over in his oilskin.

"Then why the hell do you think any less of her love? Would you consign her to a life with a man she hardly knows, bearing his children, barely tolerating his touch? If you love her so much, why don't you want her happiness above all?"

"She won't be happy without a title."

"Gammon, that's Lady Westcott speaking, not Felicia." He tried to snap his fingers, but they were too wet to make a sound. "That," he said anyway, "for Lady Westcott's ambitions. Her daughter's wishes should come first. Besides, titles are not as thick on the ground here in the country, and Lady Westcott says she wants Felicia nearby. Dash it, all they have to do is speak to Goldy Flint on your behalf. He's getting Prinny to hand out knighthoods as if they were ices from Gunther's."

"What about the marquis, then?"

"Westcott's desperate for a trustworthy estate manager, someone he can leave in charge while he rids the countryside of anything that walks, runs, flies, or crawls. He was relieved, I swear to you, to see the back of me. Felicia is a fine girl, much too good for a ne'er-do-well like me, and he knew it. I'd have made her life a misery, Johnny, without even trying. You'll try every minute of your life to see to her care and comfort. That's the way it should be."

Johnny finally rode off, grinning like a May Day fool instead of a sodden ex-soldier. "Kiss the bride for me," Kerry shouted after him. "And stay the night if they'll put you up. The roads were already getting treacherous when I came through."

The dowager had left a message with Cobb. She was going into Farley with Goldy to see the printer about wedding invitations. If she was not back that evening, he was not to worry, as Sir Goldy forecast the storm continuing. They might be forced to stay overnight at the inn there.

How nonsensical for them to set out under such conditions, Kerry thought, and how marvelously wicked. He raised his glass of hot spiced wine in salute. "Good for them!"

"Yes, I think it will be," Lucy agreed. "And I believe Felicia and Johnny will be very well pleased with each other."

"So that just leaves me and my mountain of mortgages. Any other heiresses I should cultivate? Other than the Prudlow girls, by George. I am not desperate enough for that."

"Perhaps now is a good time to speak about the second earl?"

"Is it a sad story?"

"Of course it is. How do you think he came to be a ghost otherwise?"

Kerry sipped from his glass. "Then I don't want to hear it. Not tonight. Tonight is for celebrating."

Lucinda was as relieved as the earl at his narrow escape from marriage to Felicia, so she did not press the topic. Not tonight.

Tonight, with the sound of the rain against the windows and the fire burning brightly, Lord Stanford taught Lucy how to play chess. He laughed uproariously at her efforts to move the pieces, before shifting the ivory men according to her instructions. Then she bested him at Concentration, for he couldn't concentrate on matching pairs at all, not when he was studying her instead of the cards.

Lucy was in near white tonight, with just a tinge of blush. Her gown seemed to be made of layer upon layer of some gossamer stuff that shimmered as she moved, showing baby roses strewn here and there. Another rosebud nestled in spun-gold curls clustered around her face, which was thinner now, more finely drawn. And her eyes that were once a siren's mermaid-green were now spring-soft and gold-flecked, with the innocence of a fawn. She was the most beautiful creature he had ever seen, more beautiful even than the Lucy who'd first appeared to him like a figment of his richest, most sensual imagination. He stared and stared, trying to absorb every facet of her incredible loveliness.

He never knew that, later, Lucy watched him sleep, memorizing him in turn.

A huge crash woke the earl. That and his bed shaking beneath him. The roof of the east wing had finally collapsed under the pressure of the incessant wall of water beating down on it. Kerry and Cobb took lanterns, but the passageways were too dangerous to investigate. Who knew when walls might cave in on them or floors give out? There was nothing to be done about it now, at any rate, and they could just as easily assess the damage in the morning, when the rain must eventually stop.

Unable to get back to sleep and already damp from his excursion to the disaster area, Kerry decided to check on the stable. With the head groom half deaf and the old coach driver half dead and the young grooms likely in the village with the workmen, there was no one left to calm the horses made nervous by the crash. The carriage horses were fast asleep, and the pony and mare were placidly chewing their hay, but Hellraker was kicking his stall's door and pounding against the side walls. The stallion's upset was not helped by the imbecilic pup's frenzied barking.

Those two were never going to settle, Kerry decided, so he may as well go check the pigs. He had no idea what he could do if the sows were agitated over the storm, but he saddled Hellraker, donned an oilskin coat, and took up a lantern.

The trails and paths were much worse, if they were passable at all. It was as if every brook and stream in all of Wiltshire were overflowing its banks, right onto the earl's land. The winter crop was a foot underwater, washed away. The major road was a quagmire, unsafe for man or beast, where it wasn't swept away altogether or blocked with fallen tree limbs. No one would be coming back from the village this night.

Hellraker cleared every obstacle, of course, and leapt muddy rivers as if they were puddles. But the dog got left behind, barking. "Go on home," Kerry shouted. "I'm not fishing you out of any more watery graves." But the dog kept barking and Hellraker balked at the next downed tree, almost sending Kerry flying over his head. "Hell and damnation!" he swore, but went back for the mongrel. He tucked Lucky under the oilskin coat and tightened the belt around him, because he had no free hand, what with the reins and the lantern. "Hang on!" he ordered, and sent the horse forward again.

He could hear the hogs long before he could see them, squealing like banshees even over the storm's din. Nervous, hell, the sows were frightened out of their wits, and rightfully so. Half their enclosures were underwater, and what dry ground was left was shrinking fast.

The earl was too stunned to curse. His collateral, his future, was about to float away. He didn't even know if pigs could swim, but he knew this wasn't the time to find out, not in a raging cyclone of a storm. The water had to be rechanneled away, back to the drainage ditch which, devil take it, was not complete. Or the pigs had to be gotten to higher ground. There was the barn where the fodder was kept, but it was a long, muddy field away. In the dark.

The earl wasn't a praying man. He didn't approve of those folks who petitioned the Almighty for help when it served their purposes, and ignored Him otherwise. So "Lucy!" he cried. "Where are you. I need a miracle!"

Miracles were about as common as hen's teeth that night. Lucy didn't come, and the situation was not improving for the earl's sitting there looking at it. He believed, in fact, that the water had visibly risen in the brief time since his arrival. Surely the pigs' caterwauling was louder as their feet got wetter.

Think, Kerry, think, he told himself. Then he told himself not to waste time on fruitless ventures, just do *something*. Anything. So he rode for the old barn until even Hellraker had trouble lifting his mighty hooves out of the swamp that used to be a productive field. Kerry got down and walked, pulling the horse along after him. Two lanterns hung by the barn's sagging door, so he lit both and surveyed his resources after releasing Lucky and tying Hellraker to the crossbeams. Windfall apples, a corn crib, shovels, bales of hay and straw. Everything he needed to keep his investment warm and fed, could he but get the wretched beasts there. Then he noticed the unused lumber piled near the far wall.

He didn't have time to build a raft, by Jupiter, so he'd better build a bridge. Struggling with planks taller than himself, boards that took two men to maneuver, Kerry proceeded to lay them end to end through the field. They sank nicely into the mud, making a wet but firm surface, except they were not going far enough fast enough. Working frantically, the earl lashed some of the boards together and hitched the line to Hellraker's saddle, calling in his chits.

"You owe me," he yelled at the affronted stallion, "for all the clothes you ruined." At the next trip: "And this is for my broken nose." The black snorted as he slowly picked his way along the laid planks, dragging yet another load behind him, his eyes rolling and ears well back. "And for making me a laughingstock in front of the neighbors," urged the earl.

The last plank was in place, but nowhere near the pigs. Kerry raced back to the barn and grabbed the door off its hinges. In a fury to match the storm's, he used a shovel to pry apart the door's boards, then ran with them back to his makeshift catwalk. Pigwalk.

Almost there. The rear door, a loose-box partition, finally a scattered bale of straw with his oilskin coat thrown on top, and his pigs could hie their little trotters across the mud into the safe and dry barn. He stood gasping for breath, waiting for them to arrive. And waited some more. "Apples," he called. "I've got nice apples for you." Then he cursed. "What, you bastards want stuffed grapes? Or maybe a formal invitation?"

Yelling didn't work, coaxing had no effect whatsoever, and pushing simply succeeded in getting his face flicked with the least appetizing aspect of a hog. Picking up a piglet under each arm and running like a veritable Noah would take Noah's forty days and forty nights, if Kerry could catch the wet, frantic little shoats. And the sows just grunted unhappily. Visions of Tige Welford's trampled body raced through the earl's mind. What an ignominious ending for a peer of the realm, getting ground into the mud by a rasher of ham.

That was when Kerry made an important discovery. Not that the lack of knowledge had bothered him any, but he finally realized what the mongrel hound's other half must have been. One of the mutt's ancestors had to have been the finest sheepdog in all of Britain. If not sheep, then cows or even geese. Kerry didn't care, Lucky could herd pigs!

If every dog had its day, this was Lucky's night. The little dog was running behind the nearest sow, barking and snapping at her heels, getting her moving, keeping her on the wooden pathway. Her babies followed after. Soon there was a line of pigs from the pens to the barn marching single file to the orders of one small yipping cur. Kerry's contribution was in picking up the piglets that slipped off the track into the mire and setting them back on the planks. Between times he ran to the barn to spread more straw, hay, and apples, and settle disputes over which family group claimed which stall or corner of the barn. He was bitten, scratched, and stepped on before Lucky chased the last sow and her brood across the threshold. If there were any stragglers, Kerry could not see them in the darkness, but he'd saved his bacon! He could go home.

He left Lucky guarding his new charges, the dog being too exhausted to complain, and rode out with Hellraker along the planks. And that's when he made another important discovery: the planks were no longer sitting in mud, they were underwater. The floods were still rising, and getting closer and closer to the barn. "No!" Kerry shouted into the stormswept night before his lantern went out.

Chapter Twenty-four

"*No!*" Kerry raged again when he finally reached the Abbey. The rain hadn't let up and no help had returned. Hermes knew how many porkers he'd already lost, but they'd all be gone by morning at this rate, if they weren't already chilled and sickening.

"It isn't fair!" he ranted, shaking his fist at Lucy, who sat desolate on the window seat in the library, staring at the sheets of rain. "I worked so hard, as hard as I ever could. And for what? I tried, Lucy, you know how dashed hard I tried to do things right, to be a 'good' man. Look what good it has done me!"

He tossed his wineglass into the hearth, only fractionally satisfied by the shattering crystal. "Where's the justice, Lucy? Where's the reward for good behavior? You were so busy looking for a code of conduct, an eternal truth. Well, I'll tell you how life really operates: by the law of the jungle, that's how. Dog eat dog. The strong prey on the weak. Winner takes all. And I lost, Lucy."

"But you didn't, Kerry. You can't know—"

"Oh, I know I'm sounding like a petulant child sent early to bed when his older brother gets to stay up longer, but it's so deuced cruel to have come so close and see it all washed away. And do not, if you have any sympathy for me at all, tell me that nobody promised that life was fair."

"Perhaps this is just a test, you know, like Job?"

"To see how much punishment I can take before I throw in my hand? What's next, locusts? Or was it boils? No matter, I fail. I fold. I quit. As soon as the rain stops, I'll be on my way back to London and my life of indolence. There's a lot to be said for pleasure-seeking, Lucy. You should try it sometime. Parties and plays, races and drunken revels. Elegant clothes that don't get ruined the minute you step out the door. And women. Oh, yes, women. Females I can pay in pound notes and pearls, not with my title and freedom."

"You cannot mean that, Kerry. You were much happier here, with a sense of purpose and accomplishment."

This time he threw his fist at the fireplace, and derived little more satisfaction at the pain. "I mean it, Lucy. All I've accomplished is to give people a false sense of hope. You, too. So after I leave, you can go to your friends and *you* can be the one to complain of the injustice, that they linked your fate with a hopeless libertine. You never had a chance, poor innocent, and for that I am sorry, but I'm getting out of here."

He left, but not for London. He went back out into the storm as soon as he had dry clothes and hot coffee. Wishing the pony cart stood a chance of getting through, the earl had to be content with loading more lanterns, a pistol, and some sacks on Hellraker's still-damp back. He may as well fetch home breakfast before he left, Kerry told himself. And he couldn't leave Lucky out there after the dog's valiant efforts, especially when he knew the mutt couldn't swim.

The ride took even longer this time, the stallion being almost spent. Hellraker still didn't like getting his feet wet though, so they got there, and the old barn was still standing.

And they were not alone. Everyone was there, the laboring footmen, the young grooms, his tenants new and old, Johnny and some men in Westcott's livery, Ned from the pub and Charlie the blacksmith. Even the vicar was filling grain sacks with dirt and handing them down the line to be placed around the old barn's foundation. Some of the men were lifting Kerry's gangplank and carrying the lumber to shore up the drainage ditch; others were busy with shovels, excavating new riverbeds for the water to fill.

Over Lucky's joyful greeting, Kerry swore he heard harp music, slightly out of tune.

And lilacs. The sound of harps and the smell of lilacs. And a wet, cold nose in his ear.

"Get off the bed, damn you." The earl pushed Lucky away. "Just because I said you could sleep upstairs where it was warm didn't mean my bed, you boneheaded mutt. You weren't that much of a hero!"

Lucky wagged his tail and bounded off. Kerry opened his eyes. The sun was in them; Derek must have been in earlier to open the curtains. And put flowers in his room? Not even Derek would go so far. Besides, lilacs in November? He raised his head.

Lucy was at the foot of his bed, bathed in the sun's glow so that he had to squint to get a good look at her. She was all in white, adding to the glare, and she was trailing flowers. She was smiling like the cat in the cream pot, dimples and all.

"All right, so I stayed," he grumbled. "Don't get

your hopes up. I may still leave when the roads dry out."

She shook her head and smiled fondly. "No, I am the one who is leaving. I came to say good-bye."

Kerry sat up, then pulled the covers over his bare chest when he saw her look away. "What do you mean, leaving? You can't go yet. Why—"

"But my time is up, my lord. You knew I was only here for a short time."

"But your job is not done yet! I have no heir, no wife waiting to be fruitful and multiply the Somerfield brood."

"You'll find the perfect girl in time. I've seen how you love children, and how Diccon and the little French cousins idolized you. You'll be a fine father."

"No, I'll have a relapse without you here as my conscience. I'll . . . I'll get foxed and seduce both the Prudlow granddaughters."

Lucinda laughed. "You'd have to be very cast-away indeed."

"I'll return to London on the instant, I swear," he tried in desperation.

"No, you love the land and people here now. You'll stay and see them bloom under your care. Then you'll return to London when it's time to take your seat to speak out against poverty and climbing boys and cast-off veterans."

Kerry ran his hands through his uncombed curls. "Lucy, you can't go yet! I'm no paragon of virtue. Goddamn it, I'm not," he shouted as proof.

"No, you are not," she agreed with a little laugh, "but you do have a good heart that will see you through anything. You don't need me anymore."

"Then stay because I want you, not because I need you. Please."

"I would stay if I could, you must know that, Kerry, but I have no choice."

Kerry tried to dredge up more convincing arguments, but he knew he was wasting his time. That glow around her didn't come from the sun; it was still raining. And Lucy's radiant smile wasn't because he was half naked in bed, or because he saved the pigs.

"Oh, Lucy," he sighed.

"It's better that I go now anyway," she said, trying to cheer him. "You know I couldn't have borne the time when the piglets had to go to market."

He did manage a smile at that, the slightest lifting of his lips. "Whatever shall I do without you?"

"You might try talking to the second earl. He really has a fascinating tale about when the east wing was built."

"To hell with the east wing and the second earl! They're both rubble by now."

"Kerry, don't be angry. You'll forget in time."

"Never!" he swore.

"Then remember the best times, that's what I shall do. How you taught me to waltz, and gave me my first curricle ride, and how handsome you looked riding Hellraker the first time."

"With my nose broken? That was a good time? I always said you had some devilish queer notions."

She laughed. "Then what are your best times?"

The earl thought a moment before saying: "Your smile when we waltzed, and your delight when you were up in the curricle, and how beautiful you looked when I first met you." He could not speak past the lump in his throat. He paused, swallowed. "But mostly how you look today. Perfect."

"Because of you and your goodness. You wanted so badly to show me the pleasures of life, and you succeeded. I would have no happy memories to treasure without you."

"Dash it, Lucy, I only wanted to corrupt you, at first. And if you're so happy, why are there tears on your cheeks?"

"Why are there tears on yours?" she answered softly.

He fumbled for a handkerchief on the bedstand and impatiently brushed at his eyes. "Soot from the chimney. We never did get the thing properly cleaned."

She sniffled. "Me, too."

"Oh, God, Lucy, I cannot bear to say good-bye. You are like a part of me, the best part of me."

"I know. You are the song that sings in my heart."

He gave a watery chuckle. "Off-key." Then he reached out, trying to touch her. She stretched her hand out toward him.

"Perhaps we'll meet again," she whispered.

"Do you think so?"

"I'll pray that it be. Farewell, my dearest. I will always love you."

Their fingers almost met. Almost.

Chapter Twenty-five

"What do you mean, barging into Fairview Manor like this? I won't have any havey-cavey doings, even if you brought along a man of the cloth. Our own vicar's already come and gone."

"Gone?" Lord Stanford cried out. "Lucy's not. . . ? She couldn't be, I would have known somehow."

"Lucy?" Sir Malcolm Faire demanded. "Do you mean my daughter Lucinda, sirrah?"

"She lives?" It was all he could do not to take the older man's scrawny neck between his hands and shake him until his teeth rattled. "Tell me she lives!"

Sir Malcolm sneered. "She lives. Though how it concerns a here-and-thereian like yourself is beyond reason." He surveyed his caller's gleaming Hessians, the high shirt collar, and embroidered waistcoat. "What could a London fribble"—he consulted the calling card still in his hand—"like the Earl of Stanford have to do with that miserable wench upstairs who refuses to let go her hold on the thinnest thread of life?"

At the shocked inhalation of the vicar at Kerry's

side, Sir Malcolm ground out: "Oh, I make no bones about it. Why wear the cloak of hypocrisy when everyone in the country knows the girl's a wanton, and a murderess besides? The London papers must have given you every sordid detail of my disgrace, so you'd do better to wonder why I even bother with the trappings of mourning." He waved at the crepe-hung mirrors, the black clothes he wore. "It's so the prying neighbors leave me alone in my supposed grief! People with more courtesy than you stay away." He turned to ring for a footman to show them the door. "I say the sooner the girl is in the ground, the sooner my shame can be put behind me."

"But, sir, she is your daughter!"

"She is no get of mine!" Sir Malcolm thundered.

The urge to murder the man grew even stronger in Kerry's breast. Only the knowledge that time was running out, that it had taken too long to get to Derby, the roads were so bad, made him refrain. He took a deep breath. Nodding toward the card Sir Malcolm had tossed aside, he reiterated: "I am Kieren Somerfield, Earl of Stanford. I have brought a vicar and a special license, and I have come to marry your daughter."

"What?" Sir Malcolm gasped, growing red of face. "That's outrageous! What perversion is this, with the girl at death's door? And you"—he turned to the vicar—"how could you be part of this blasphemy?"

Kerry answered. "There is no blasphemy, Sir Malcolm, no vile motives. My word as a gentleman."

"Your word? Why should I accept your word, my fancy lord? Oh, yes, I know you by reputation. I wouldn't have let a rakehell like you near Lucinda in the best of times."

"But you'd let that old nipcheese Halbersham near her?" Kerry spat out.

"How did you know about that? It wasn't in any of the London scandal sheets."

"I know. I cannot explain how, but I know it all. Do I have your permission?"

"No, blast you! I know your sort, gamesters and wastrels all. Here you are, dressed to the nines, your nose in the air, and run off your feet. You saw your salvation in the gossip columns and you've come to make a deathbed marriage to a poor, unfortunate heiress. Well, you shan't have the wench, nor a shilling of my money!"

Kerry clenched his fists so tightly, his nails cut through his palms. "If you know my sort, you know I am arrogant and overbearing and used to getting my own way. Pigheaded to a fault. And I wish to marry your daughter for reasons I could never explain and you could never understand. But none of them have to do with your blunt."

Sir Malcolm snorted, unconvinced.

"What did your wealth ever give to Lucy when she was alive and well? Did it buy her pretty dresses and gay parties? Friends her own age or lovesick mooncalfs writing odes to her eyebrows? No. You were so afraid of fortune hunters you kept her from having any of the pleasures a young girl deserves!"

Sir Malcolm looked away, but Kerry persisted: "Your money never made her happy, so keep it now, old man. I do not want a groat from you, only Lucy."

"A wager, that's it, isn't it? It's not my brass you want, it's some other scapegrace's fortune you hope to win. That's why a rackety London buck like you is here offering for a dying girl with no reputation." He nodded to himself, like a vulture bobbing over a carcass.

"If there was a wager, it wasn't mine. Can't you believe I have nothing to gain, except Lucy as my wife? If you have any human feeling at all, let me give her my name. Let me restore her honor in the only way I can."

"Honor, what honor? She has none."

Kerry ignored the other's outburst. "I cannot kill that makebait who ran off with her, for he's already got his just desserts. And I shall not call out a man old enough to be my father, although you tempt me, Sir Malcolm, you really do."

Lucy's father took a step closer to the bellpull. The vicar clucked his teeth.

"Stop, Sir Malcolm," Kerry ordered. "Stop and listen. You know marriage to a peer, any peer, even one below the hatches, restores a girl's reputation. Let me give her my name while there is still time. You don't even want her. You've practically disowned her. So let her come with me. She'll lie with my family in Wiltshire; you won't even have a footstone to remind you that you ever had a daughter."

"And you say you won't make any claim on her portion?"

"If she lives, sign it over to our children."

"Lives? My word, the man is madder than I thought! The physician says it's a miracle she's held on so long. He swears she won't last till dawn."

"Let it be on your head if she dies disgraced. I'll worry about her living."

Kerry had another skirmish on his hands, this time with Lucinda's old nanny, whose gaunt frame blocked the door.

"You cannot come in here. This is a sacrilege, wedding with a woman you never even met."

"But I do know her, ma'am, maybe the way one knows a dream or a figure from a novel, or . . . or a vision. I have no explanation to give you, just that I do know her. I know she is the sweetest, most loving person on earth, and she is being killed by unkindness. And the world would be a poorer place without her in it."

"But my lamb is going to die. I did all I could, spooning broth into her despite *his* orders, but she won't wake up." Nanny brought her apron up to wipe her eyes. "The doctor says it's too late now. She never will."

Kerry's eyes were damp, too. "Then at least I shall honor her memory by recalling all the good she has done, and placing flowers on her grave. She loves flowers, did you know?"

They held the wedding as soon as Nanny threaded some ribbon through Lucinda's shorn curls and got a footman to fetch a bouquet from the indoor gardener.

The Earl of Stanford took Miss Lucinda Faire to be his lawful wife, with two servants as witnesses, Sir Malcolm and his lady being otherwise engaged. Kerry stroked Lucy's limp, emaciated hand and Nanny made the bride's responses, until she got to the part about till death do us part. The vicar had to pause and wipe his spectacles while Nanny wept into her apron.

It was done.

Then Kerry sent Nanny off to bring hot soups, lemonade, sweetened tea. He climbed onto the bed beside Lucy's still form, gathered her frail body into his arms, and began the final battle.

"Hello, angel," he murmured into her ear. "Do you remember me? I'm Kerry, the one who loves you. And you love me. You told me so, do you recall? Don't worry, I'll keep reminding you. I never did get the chance to tell you, my darling, because you left just when I was discovering that I had a heart after all.

"You thought I could live without you, didn't you? You said I'd be fine, but you were wrong. I won't be fine at all. Oh, I won't drink myself into oblivion more than two or three times a week, and I won't return to my licentious ways, because you showed me how empty those passing pleasures are. I won't even fall into mercenary habits, for you showed me things of infinite value, which will be as ashes without you. I'll live, Lucy, but I will not be fine, I will not be complete. If you left, I'd have only half a life, for I need you, sweetheart, to show me the good in everything, to show me the rainbows, to fill those aching voids. I cannot be happy without you, Lucy. And you do care about my happiness, I know you do, for it was you who taught me about caring." He paused to kiss her reed-thin fingers.

"And you must love me very much, for you waited until I got here. Did you know I would come after you? I wish you'd done something about the wretched roads, then." He tried to smile, and tried to get some broth into her. He was awkward, especially with her still in his hold, leaning back against his chest, but he would not put her down or let Nanny wield the spoon. He tucked another towel under Lucy's chin and kept speaking softly.

"Do you remember me now? I am Kerry, the one who loves you. Do you recall when we met and you told me you had no reason to live? Let me be the reason, angel. And our children and the life we can have together. We'll fix up the Abbey. It might take decades, but who knows, we might find another Diccon whose parents will help restore the old pile. And I'll show you all the good parts of London when Goldy and my mother aren't staying in Grosvenor Square. You'll make a splash in the ton, love, in your silks and satins, but I won't let that horde of beaus too near you. I mean to be a doting husband. Very well," he said as though she made comment, "you can call it a jealous husband. Oh, did I tell you that we are married? I didn't even forget the ruby this time, but the ring is too big, so it's back in my pocket. We'll have to fatten you up like the piglets, *mon ange*. And we'll keep every one of the little oinkers if you want. I'll never eat bacon again, I swear."

He fed her some more broth, massaging her throat while she swallowed.

"Do you remember now? No matter, you can hear me, I'm positive, so I'll just keep repeating it until you decide to wake up, my sleeping beauty." But first he kissed her as softly as a butterfly on her dry lips, as if she really were a sleeping princess who could be awakened by a broken-nosed earl who needed a shave. Or as if he would share his very breath with her, the kiss of life.

Kerry talked all night until he was hoarse and after, spooning liquid into her when he could, gently rubbing warmth into her wraithlike limbs.

He told her about the devil's wager and the angel's bargain, about his wicked life and her innocence. He spoke of Demby's lottery and Lucky's near drowning, of the hidden paintings and hiding the fox up a tree. Begging her to remember, the earl related how she made him see the good in Goldy Flint, and the importance of love in Johnny and Felicia.

When he was finished he started over, whispering of his great love for her, his desperate need of her. "I am Kerry, the one who loves you. . . ."

Near dawn, Lucinda's eyes fluttered open. "Nanny?" she called in a voice that was raspy from disuse. She sipped from a glass held to her lips. "Nanny, I had the strangest dream about—why, you're not Nanny," she croaked. "You . . . you're Kerry, aren't you?"

With tears streaming down his cheeks, Kerry tried not to hug her delicate body. "Yes, angel. I am Kerry."

"The one who loves me." It was a fact, not a question.

He managed a shaky laugh. "More than life itself. And you love me, wife," he stated just as firmly.

"More than my hope of heaven." Her brows knit. "But I don't remember any wedding."

"You slept through the first one, so we'll have another as soon as you are strong, darling. At the Abbey with all of our friends."

"Yes, I would like that." Her trembling hand was reaching out to touch his beloved face, his only slightly crooked nose. "Ah, I have been waiting a lifetime to do that. But, Kerry, you are not the man in my dreams."

Kerry's arms stiffened and his jaw tightened. "I'm not?"

"No, he was a funny old man dressed for a masquerade in scarlet tights."

The earl relaxed. "Oh, him. I forgot about the second earl. We'll invite him to the wedding, too, angel."

"But he only wants to tell you about your treasure," she insisted drowsily.

"I'm holding the only thing that is precious, dear heart, and I will cherish it forever." He lowered her back to the pillows, but sat on the bed beside her. "You rest now and we'll talk later."

"But you really have to know."

"I do, I swear. I know all about my treasure, Lucy."

"Oh, good, then you won't tear up the east wing until you find that sack of gold."